Where were *you* when the clock struck twelve?

Maggie Kelley planned to ring in the new millennium by announcing her engagement. Only, at the stroke of midnight, she found herself in the arms of the wrong man....

Luke Fitzpatrick, Maggie's childhood hero, should have been happy she's found the man of her dreams. So why is he itching to punch out the groom?

Colin Spencer, heir to the Spencer fortune, has finally chosen a bride. But he hadn't counted on the millennium bug—and sexy Isabelle Channing—to wreak havoc on his well-ordered world....

Isabelle Channing, the bride-to-be's best friend, can't just stand by and let Maggie make the biggest mistake of her life. And she doesn't....

Four lives. Four loves.
One date with destiny.

Dear Reader,

Welcome to the year 2000! It's a brand-new century and Harlequin Temptation is ready to celebrate. We've got two fabulous linked stories by fan favorite Kate Hoffmann, both set on the most romantic night of the year.

New Year's Eve. December 31, 1999. It's the eve of the new millennium. Legend says the person you're with at the stroke of midnight is "the one." So what happens when Maggie Kelley finds herself *not* with fiancé Colin...but in the arms of her sexy childhood hero Luke? Find out in #758, *Once a Hero*. The fun continues in January with #762, *Always a Hero,* when the unpredictable Isabelle Channing, Maggie's best friend, also finds herself with the wrong man at midnight!

I hope you enjoy both of these great books. As a treat for our overseas readers, the books will be published around the world at the same time as in North America. Truly, love can be a universal experience!

Lastly, I hope you have exciting plans to celebrate the millennium. Whether it's an elegant party, a trip to Hawaii or just curling up by the fire with a Temptation novel, I hope the new century brings you love, peace and happiness.

Warmly,

Birgit Davis-Todd
Senior Editor
Harlequin Temptation

Kate Hoffmann
ONCE A HERO

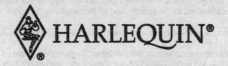

HARLEQUIN®

TORONTO • NEW YORK • LONDON
AMSTERDAM • PARIS • SYDNEY • HAMBURG
STOCKHOLM • ATHENS • TOKYO • MILAN • MADRID
PRAGUE • WARSAW • BUDAPEST • AUCKLAND

ISBN 0-373-25858-5

ONCE A HERO

Copyright © 1999 by Peggy Hoffmann.

Dear Reader,

It's hard to remember an event that has so captured the world's attention. One tick of a clock and, except for that little time zone problem, all of us will be celebrating the same event—the year 2000—at the same time!

When I came up with the ideas for *Once a Hero* and *Always a Hero,* my senior editor, Birgit Davis-Todd, mentioned that the books would be released worldwide at the same time. It didn't hit me until I started writing this reader letter that we'll have a chance to celebrate the millennium together, between the covers of these books.

Readers all over the world will be turning pages at the same time, wondering what will happen to Luke and Maggie...and Colin and Isabelle. Proving once again that no matter what our differences, love will always bring us together.

So, I offer a toast to all my readers—may the new millennium bring you health and happiness, and most especially, love.

Happy New Year,

Kate Hoffmann

For my readers all over the world.

1

EVERY LIGHT IN THE CITY had been turned on to ring in the New Year. Fifty-one stories above Michigan Avenue, Maggie Kelley stared out into the night. From her vantage point, the city of Chicago looked like a lush, black carpet strewn with precious jewels, stretching all the way to the horizon. She caught sight of a falling star and made a quick wish, then realized it was only a plane descending over O'Hare.

No matter, she mused. All her wishes were about to come true anyway. Drawing her gaze from the window, she glanced down at her left hand. A huge diamond winked back at her, catching the light from the chandeliers above. In just sixty minutes, her destiny would be sealed. And it would begin at the exact moment the new millennium did.

"New Year's resolution number one," she murmured, twisting the ring around her finger. "I will marry Colin Spencer and be deliriously happy."

As resolutions went, it was a big one, especially when it involved an entire lifetime. But she'd been planning for this moment for as long as she could remember. Colin would make a wonderful husband. He was kind and attentive, brilliant and driven. His financial situation would give her the security and stability she'd always craved. And his socially prominent family, though a bit intimidating at times, had welcomed her with just the proper amount of warmth and enthusiasm.

Maggie sighed. Maybe asking for complete happiness was a bit greedy. After all, she was the only child of Marlene Pritchard Kelley...Olmgren Dumbrowski Schmidt Mooney. There were a few other names that belonged on the end of the string, but Maggie had stopped keeping track after she left home at eighteen. Her mother had collected enough marriage certificates and divorce decrees to wallpaper the village hall in her tiny hometown of Potter's Junction in northern Wisconsin. Maggie knew better than anyone that marriage was a risky proposition.

She pressed her palm against the cold glass and took one last look at the city below. "So it's not all passion and romance with Colin," she admitted softly. "But it's better to use my head to choose a husband than my heart."

Clearing her throat and straightening her spine, Maggie looked over the huge ballroom on the top floor of the Spencer Center. Tiny lights twinkled from the ceiling and wrapped around ornate columns. Silver lamé lay draped over tables topped with fresh white orchids. A dance band played on the far end of the reception hall and an elegant buffet was laid out nearby.

All around her, Chicago's elite had turned out for the party of the year—the party of the century some would say. An invitation to Eunice Spencer's Millennium Eve Ball was as coveted to high society as Bulls tickets were to a Windy City sports fan.

Smoothing the skirt of her gown, Maggie pasted a serene smile on her face and tried to look as if she was having a good time. These society affairs always made her a little nervous. Other women drifted around the room, so calm and self-assured in their party dresses and high heels, dripping expensive jewels. But in company like this, Maggie felt like a giraffe on roller skates.

There were so many expectations involved in marrying into the Spencer family, the least of which was being able to navigate any type of social event, from polo matches to political fund-raisers. In truth, Margaret Mary Kelley was not exactly what Edward and Eunice Spencer expected in a daughter-in-law. They had expected their son to marry within their own social circle, to bring along family connections, traditions, the innate ability to walk in a pair of party shoes.

They expected a daughter-in-law who could entertain with grace and ease, and keep a luxurious home, and volunteer her time to worthwhile and trendy causes. They didn't expect a girl from the woods of northern Wisconsin, a mere shopkeeper with a small floral shop on Clark Street, a meager savings account, a one-bedroom condo in Wicker Park and a multimarried mother.

A party horn sounded in Maggie's left ear and she jumped, pressing her palm to her chest. "Isabelle!" Her friend stood there, looking amused.

"Don't look so glum. At midnight, little green aliens will descend on this party and turn all these bluebloods into pod people. It's a millennium prophecy, haven't you heard?" Isabelle Channing handed her a plate filled with tasty tidbits, fresh shrimp and stuffed pea pods and toast topped with caviar and sour cream. "This food is to die for. Old Eunice sure knows how to put out a spread."

Grateful for the diversion, Maggie stuffed a shrimp into her mouth and munched intently. "Have you noticed? None of these women eat. That's one more thing I'll have to master. Sophisticated starvation."

Isabelle tapped her brightly manicured index finger on her lips as she considered the observation. "Maybe they're already pod people. Pod people don't eat. And they do look a little…vacuous."

Maggie giggled. "Compared to you, *everyone* looks a little lifeless."

A mischievous smile curled Isabelle's lushly stained lips. "Thank you. I'm glad at least one person appreciates my gown." She posed dramatically. "I designed it myself."

As always, Isabelle had chosen to wear something that caused heads to turn and mouths to gape. An outrageous fashion sense was just one of the things Maggie loved about her friend. Tonight, Is wore a crimson gown of Egyptian influence, with bold designs and intricate beading and a neckline cut down to her waist. Her dark hair was slicked back and knotted at her nape and her eyes were rimmed with kohl. She looked like a modern-day version of Cleopatra, quite appropriate for a woman who most recently designed the costumes for the Shakespeare Theatre Company's production of *Antony and Cleopatra*.

Maggie glanced down at the sedate gown she'd chosen, an ice-blue satin sheath with a conservative neckline, a gown that complemented her pale hair and complexion and hid all her figure flaws. A gown she'd chosen more for comfort and practicality than beauty. There were moments when she wished she could be as audacious as Isabelle, that she had the courage to wear outrageous colors and sexy designs. Maybe that's why they'd become such quick friends—they were polar opposites.

"You obviously haven't resolved to start dressing conservatively for the new millennium," Maggie teased.

"Oh, no," Isabelle replied. "But I did make a few other resolutions. I've resolved to give up topless bathing on North Beach. And I won't be mouthing off to policemen in the next year. I've also decided to stop dating policemen who arrest me for indecent exposure."

Maggie giggled. "Anything else?"

"Yeah, I'm giving up chocolate."

Maggie and Isabelle had known each other for nearly four years, since the night they'd met in a watercolor class at the Art Institute. The notion of having a close girlfriend had been completely foreign to Maggie. As a child and a teenager, she had never had time for girlfriends. She'd been too busy serving as her mother's confidante, coddling her through another divorce or feigning joy at an upcoming marriage.

She'd been the grown-up in the family, the practical, levelheaded member who worried about the electricity bills and made the grocery lists and cleaned up the mess after another one of her mother's short-lived marriages. Marlene Kelley had quite a reputation in and around Potter's Junction, a reputation that had followed Maggie around as well.

Her teachers had whispered and her schoolmates had taunted her. She'd been too shy and afraid to change their opinions, so Maggie had stood on the sidelines, an outsider without a friend to her name. Except for Luke, of course. Luke Fitzpatrick had become her hero, her white knight. Three years older and an outsider himself, he was the only person in Potter's Junction who had bothered to stand up for Maggie, no matter how big the bully or how frightening the mob of kids. Luke had always been there to protect her, like the big brother she'd never had.

"Did you come with Luke?" Maggie asked.

Isabelle shook her head. "He was supposed to bring me, but he's off to some war zone tomorrow. He had to pack and pick up his airline tickets. He said he'd try to make it."

Maggie and Luke were still best friends, after all these years. It hadn't been by chance that Maggie had ended up in the same city as Luke. She'd planned her escape from Potter's Junction for years, and the day after graduating from high school, she'd hopped a Greyhound and left Marlene Kelley in the capable care of her latest husband.

Maggie's destination had never been in question. After she arrived in Chicago, Luke had helped her find a job and encouraged her to enroll in college. By the time she'd moved off his couch and into an apartment of her own, she'd managed to put together a whole new life for herself—a life that brought her to this point on the eve of the millennium.

Maggie squeezed her friend's hand, then tucked it into the crook of her elbow. "I take it things aren't going too well with you two?"

"I think I make him crazy," Isabelle replied after taking a long sip of her champagne. "We have an occasional date but I know he sees other women. Of course, I haven't mentioned that I see other men. Neither one of us is looking for a commitment."

Maggie winced inwardly. When she'd introduced Luke and Isabelle, she'd hoped they might find some happiness together. It had seemed like a sensible plan. After all, Luke had introduced her to Colin—his frat brother from his days at Northwestern—two years earlier, so she'd felt compelled to return the favor. Unfortunately, Isabelle's assessment was right. Luke wasn't the kind to marry and raise a family. That had been Maggie's dream and hers alone.

Maggie wasn't sure why she wanted Luke settled and happy. Maybe it was guilt. After all, Colin was supposed to be the most important man in her life, not Luke. In just a short time, she'd be a Spencer, a wife with little time to devote to an old friend—a male friend at that. Still, she didn't want to desert Luke, to leave him without a confidante.

But then, for the past couple of years, Luke had been pulling away, spending much more time than he used to out of the country on assignment. When they did get together, they barely had time to talk, not the way they always had. The change in their relationship had come gradually, but Maggie could trace it almost to the day she started dating Colin.

Maybe he'd never settle down. Luke's job as a journalist for an international press syndicate didn't really leave room for a relationship or even a personal life. He loved to be in the middle of the action, wherever bullets flew and mortars exploded. First the Persian Gulf, then Bosnia, and after that, any revolution in Eastern Europe. Now he was off to another battle zone on the other side of the world.

"So what resolutions did you make?" Isabelle asked, her gaze fixed on a handsome man across the room. They made eye contact and Isabelle gave him a little wave and a coy smile. "You're never without one of your plans."

Maggie marveled at her friend's ability to attract men, a trait Maggie had never perfected. "I've resolved to be blissfully happy."

"Look!" Isabelle cried, clutching Maggie's arm. "Old Eunice has hired a fortune-teller. Such a radical choice for a Spencer affair! Let's go find out what the next century holds for us."

Maggie shook her head. "I already know," she murmured.

"How can you possibly know?"

Maggie swallowed convulsively and held out her hand. The diamond looked obscenely large and she felt a momentary flash of embarrassment. Considering Isabelle's opinion of Colin and his family, she would not be enthusiastic about the news. "He asked me to marry him on Christmas Eve. I—I said yes. We're going to announce it right before midnight tonight."

Isabelle snatched up Maggie's fingers, her eyes wide, her mouth agape. "No! But—but you can't marry him! He's such a—a bore, a stuffed shirt!" She made a face like she'd just caught a whiff of something rotten. "Besides, you don't love him."

Maggie glanced around, hoping no one had overhead Isabelle's outburst. "That's not true! I care about Colin and I respect him. And—and he can give me the life I've always wanted. A future and a real family."

"A family?" Isabelle repeated. "His family? You want to be a—a pod person? A Stepford wife?"

"Colin and I will have a family of our own," she said softly. "We'll have children."

"Even if you don't love him?"

"My mother loved all her husbands and where did that get her? I'm not a passionate person, Is. I don't feel things the way you do. But that doesn't mean I can't be happy with Colin."

Isabelle sighed. "With a man you don't love?"

"I do love him!" Maggie cried. "Just because I don't dress up in Saran Wrap or dance naked on the kitchen table or send him my underwear in the mail, doesn't mean I don't love him."

"I didn't mail my underwear," Isabelle said with a pout. "I sent it Federal Express."

"And what if I don't marry him? Is someone else going to come along?" Maggie shook her head in answer to her own question. "Colin is the one. If I can't be happy with him, then I'll never be happy."

Isabelle gave her a long look, then shook her own head. "You deserve so much better. You deserve fireworks and brass bands and—"

"I don't need those things." Maggie forced a smile then stared out at the party again, searching the crowd for her future husband. "I have everything I could possibly want. I promise."

With a resigned groan, Isabelle drew her into a warm hug. "Come on. You might know what the future holds, but I don't. Let's go see that fortune-teller."

They crossed the room together, weaving through the crowd gathered near the dance floor. Eunice had put Madame Blavatka in a small alcove near the ice sculpture and she'd drawn quite a crowd with her tarot readings and crystal ball. When they reached the table, both chairs were empty and Madame was looking for a new victim. Isabelle pushed Maggie into one chair, then sat down beside her.

"You've come to hear your future," Madame Blavatka said in a heavily accented voice. She stared at Maggie with a piercing gaze and grabbed her hand.

Maggie tried to pull away but the woman had a grip of steel. "No, not me! I—I really don't believe in fortunes."

"Oh, but you should, for I see great fortune here." Her bracelets jangled against the embroidered tablecloth as she stroked Maggie's palm. Uneasy, Maggie gave Isabelle an irritated look.

Madame drew in a sharp breath, then peered more closely at Maggie's hand. "Oh, my! You have the mark of the millennium!" She drew her finger along the base of Maggie's thumb, then pointed dramatically. "See? Here it is. It's supposed to be very rare." She frowned. "Twice in one night is quite odd."

"The mark of the millennium?" Isabelle stared at Maggie's upturned hand. "Is that important?"

The fortune-teller nodded solemnly. "These small lines intersect to form a tiny star. Legend has it that any person with this mark will find the greatest love of their life, their destiny, at midnight on the millennium."

"Colin," Maggie murmured. "I'll be with Colin at midnight." She turned to Isabelle. "You see, there's no need to worry! Everything will turn out just fine. He's my destiny."

The fortune-teller smiled and continued to stroke Maggie's palm. "I see you already have a long history with this man. You've spent several lives together. He knows your deepest heart and the depths of your soul."

"He doesn't even remember her favorite color!" Isabelle cried. "Remember, he bought you that purple sweater last year for your birthday. You hate purple."

Maggie hushed her friend and turned back to the fortune-teller. "That was just one instance. He's very thoughtful."

"Oh, yes," Madame insisted. "And you see yourself in his eyes. The troubles of your past, the hopes for your future. He is your soul mate."

"Colin Spencer, a soul mate?" Isabelle sat back and laughed. "The guy doesn't have a soul! How much did Eunice Spencer pay you to say that?" She grabbed for the woman's headdress. "Do you have an earpiece in there?" She yanked up the tablecloth and looked beneath. "Who's telling you to say these things?"

Maggie gasped. "Isabelle! How could you—"

"No!" The fortune-teller held up her hand for silence. She closed her eyes and tipped her head back. "This man...your destiny...his name is..." She frowned, deep furrows wrinkling her forehead. "Not Colin."

"I knew it!" Isabelle jumped out of her seat. "I told you, Maggie. Listen to this woman. She knows what she's talking about."

Maggie snatched her hand away, rubbing her palm on the cool fabric of her skirt. She pushed up the chair and flipped open her evening bag, then tossed a tip onto the table. "I—I told you, I don't believe in fortune-tellers." She took a few wary steps back. "I—I have to find Colin. It's nearly midnight."

With that, Maggie turned and hurried away from the fortune-teller's table, suddenly desperate to have a quiet moment to herself. She needed time to think, time to reassure herself that she'd made the right choice. Colin *was* the right choice, wasn't he?

She couldn't be wrong about that, not about something so important, not about someone she'd been waiting for her entire life.

LUKE FITZPATRICK SCANNED the crowd, searching for a familiar face, one in particular. He glanced down at his watch and cursed softly. Maggie would probably chide him for his tardiness, never mind his lack of formal wear. Thirty minutes before midnight and he was only just arriving. He hadn't had time to run home and shower, or change into the tux requested on the bottom of the invitation. Jeans, topped with a shirt and tie would have to suffice. But he *had* made it for the big event, the midnight hour, the turn of the century and the new millennium.

He grabbed a glass of champagne from a passing

waiter and gulped it down, then placed the glass back on the tray. Luke probably wouldn't have come to the party at all had it not been for Maggie's personal invitation and follow-up call. She'd been so intent on his attending, he didn't want to let her down.

Odd that he put Maggie's feelings before Isabelle's. But Maggie was like family. She'd been the little sister he'd never had. Maggie Kelley could ask him to jump off the Sears Tower and he'd probably oblige. So if she requested his presence at this party, he'd do his best to please her and act as if he was enjoying himself. As for Isabelle, she was just his date and he'd never quite figured out what made her happy.

Luke had dated a lot of women, beautiful women, intelligent women. But he'd never dated a woman quite like Isabelle Channing. She was unpredictable and alluring and perplexing and incredibly beautiful. And she didn't give a damn about him—or any man for that matter. Maggie had introduced them, hoping they might become better acquainted.

Luke suspected they continued to date each other to please Maggie. Isabelle had no appreciation for his work, couldn't stand to discuss current events and would rather flip through a fashion magazine than a newspaper. As for Luke, he had no interest in the theatre, didn't understand the way she dressed and couldn't figure out why she changed her hair color every other month.

There were times when Luke wondered why he even bothered with women at all. He had no interest in a permanent relationship. The minute a woman started talking in that direction, he cut her loose. The other reason he continued to date Isabelle was that she had a lower opinion of marriage than he did.

If he were to settle down, he wouldn't choose a

woman like Isabelle, or like any of the other women he had dated. When he thought about a lifelong partner, he thought about a woman like...like Maggie. She was sweet and even-tempered and she knew him inside and out. He always felt like a better man when he was with her, as if he could accomplish anything he set his mind to. And Maggie accepted and appreciated who he really was, warts and all.

"Quite a dress, isn't it?"

"What?" Luke glanced over his shoulder and found Colin Spencer standing behind him. Colin clapped him across the back and pushed another glass of champagne into his hand, then pointed to a spot across the room. Isabelle stood there, surrounded by a group of men, keeping them all entertained with her beauty and her laughter.

Luke shook his head and chuckled. "That *is* quite a dress. And I'll bet she's not wearing a stitch of underwear beneath it."

Colin's eyes widened in what appeared to be genuine shock. Spencer had always been a little stuffy and straitlaced. Even now, after a night of pressing the flesh, the guy looked as if he'd been drinking starch instead of expensive bubbly. Luke, on the other hand, might as well have slept in his jacket and jeans. In fact, he *had* slept in his jacket and jeans last night!

"Are you two still..." Colin let his question drift off.

Luke shrugged. "We see each other every now and then. But nothing serious."

Colin continued to stare. "I can't understand what she and Maggie have in common. Isabelle Channing is—"

"Intriguing?"

Colin nodded slowly. "That, too. I was going to say dangerous."

"Take my advice, she's more trouble than she's worth," Luke said.

"Trouble," Colin murmured. "Just once I'd like to know a woman who was trouble."

Luke frowned at his friend, and jabbed him in the ribs with his elbow. "You've got something better than trouble, you've got Maggie."

Colin blinked, then drew his gaze away from Isabelle. "Yeah," he murmured. "Maggie." A hesitant smile touched his lips and he glanced around distractedly. "I better get back to mingling. If you see Maggie, would you tell her I'm looking for her?"

Luke nodded to the man beside him, confused by his friend's distracted expression. Usually, Colin was so focused, so direct. Tonight, it seemed as if he were a million miles away.

"And make sure you're here at midnight," Colin added. "We've got a big announcement."

"An announcement?"

"Huge announcement. You'll be pleased." Colin grabbed Luke's hand and gave it a halfhearted shake. "Now go get yourself something to eat. Enjoy the party."

Luke watched Colin stride across the room, dressed in a designer tux and looking every bit the scion of one of Chicago's wealthiest families. The guy had everything going for him and he didn't even realize it— money, good looks, intelligence, connections...and he also had Maggie. Luke drew in a sharp breath and pushed aside the envy that pricked his heart.

How could he help but be a little envious? Spencer had been handed all the breaks in his life. Luke had had to make his own. As for Colin's announcement, Luke knew what it would probably be. The business press had been speculating about it all year long. Colin had been positioning himself for the presidency of Spencer Enterprises since college and lately there had been talk that Edward Spencer was going to step down. What better time to turn the reins over to his only son than at the beginning of a new millennium?

Luke's attention was caught by a flash of color and a low, throaty laugh. Isabelle had made her way out to the dance floor and she now twirled and dipped around a handsome young man. Her movements were playful, yet enticing, causing those around her to stop and watch. She'd obviously had too much champagne and before long would make a total fool of herself. In a few long strides, Luke crossed the dance floor and gently tugged her out of the limelight.

Isabelle turned and wrapped her arms around his neck, pressing her slender form against his. "You're here! Dance with me, Fitzpatrick! I'm in the mood."

For the first time in recent memory, he didn't respond to her body, didn't feel an instant attraction to her touch. Maybe it was the crowd on the dance floor watching them, or maybe because she'd had too much to drink. Or perhaps he was simply anticipating the argument they'd have if he refused. "Isabelle, why don't we sit this one out."

"No," she said with a coy smile. "How do you like my dress?" She spun around in front of him and he caught her in his arms.

"I think it's…revealing. And I think you're just a little drunk." He grabbed her elbow and gently steered her off the dance floor.

"I was celebrating," she said with one of her pretty pouts. "We have something big to celebrate tonight."

"And what's that?"

Her dark eyebrow arched teasingly. "Didn't you

hear? My very best friend is going to marry your very best friend!"

Luke gasped, stunned by her revelation. His grip tightened on her arm. "What did you say?" Could that be what Colin was talking about? His big announcement?

"Don't look so surprised. They're announcing their engagement at midnight. You must have known it was coming. After all, you put the two of them together."

"Maggie is engaged to Colin?"

She nodded. "Since Christmas Eve. But it'll be official tonight." Isabelle drew her arm up and peered at her watch, then pushed it into his face. "We still have time to stop it." She stared up into his eyes, her gaze suddenly intense, as if she was searching the depths of his soul for the truth of his feelings. He glanced away as realization dawned on her face. "You want to stop it, don't you?"

Her words were more a statement of fact than a question and his first impulse was to answer, "Yes." Hell, yeah, he wanted to stop it—or at least put it on pause for a few minutes until he could figure out why he was feeling this way!

His first thought was one of pure selfishness. He felt as though he was losing something, something attached to him so tightly and deeply that he would be diminished without it. Maggie had been his best friend for so long, the thought of her depending on another man, loving another man, left a gaping hole where his heart was.

As for Colin, his rise to the top had been frustrated for years by Edward Spencer's stubborn insistence on one thing. First and foremost, Colin's father said, the president of Spencer Enterprises needed a wife. And shortly thereafter, an heir and a spare.

"Damn it," Luke muttered. "Why didn't she tell me?" Every protective instinct he possessed had kicked in and he suddenly needed to talk to Colin, needed to assure himself the guy's intentions were honorable, that he truly loved Maggie. And then he needed to find Maggie and make sure she knew what she was getting into.

"I take it you don't approve?" Isabelle asked.

Luke turned to look at her, forgetting for a moment she was still there. "If—if Maggie is happy, then I'm happy for her."

A smile curled her lushly painted lips. "Happy? Are you sure about that?"

Luke had no patience for Isabelle's little games. Right now, all he could think about was Maggie. "Have you seen her?"

Isabelle slowly stepped away from him, dropping her hands to her sides. "I think she went down to Colin's apartment." Her voice was thoughtful. "Why don't you go and find her? I'm sure you two have a lot to talk about."

Luke gave her a curt nod, then started for the door, leaving Isabelle standing alone near the dance floor. The crowd closed around her, and when he glanced back over his shoulder, she was already chatting with another admirer. He shook his head as he stepped into the foyer and started toward the elevators.

Why hadn't Maggie told him? He'd talked to her twice since Christmas Eve and she'd had plenty of opportunity to break the news. Geez, they were like family. Maggie had always discussed important decisions with him. He stopped short, then cursed softly.

What the hell was he thinking? In truth, he and Maggie had grown apart over the past couple of years—and it had been all his fault. They barely saw each other these days and rarely had time to talk for more than a few minutes. The reason he'd introduced her to Colin was that it had helped ease the guilt he felt over his busy schedule and long absences.

But he'd never expected it to go this far! Two years had flown by like two months and while he wasn't watching, Maggie had fallen in love and chosen a husband. She hadn't told him about her engagement because it wasn't any of his business! They led separate lives now, the bond between them slowly thinning until it was as fine and fragile as a spiderweb.

Luke knew he should turn around and go back to the party. He knew, for Maggie's sake, he should accept her good news with grace and enthusiasm. But something wouldn't allow him to just stand by and let this engagement happen. He needed to hear it straight from Maggie's mouth—that she loved Colin and wanted to marry him. He needed to see the certainty in her eyes.

First, he needed to talk to Colin. Luke turned and stalked into the reception hall. With a patient eye, he scanned the crowd until he found his old college buddy. Taking a straight path toward him, Luke considered what he was going to say. He'd be calm and supportive, but he'd demand the truth.

By the time he reached Colin, he'd already tossed aside that plan. "Hey, I need to talk to you."

Colin turned away from the group of men he was with and blinked in surprise. "Luke," he said. "Gentlemen, this is my old friend and fraternity brother, Luke Fitzpatrick. Luke, this is—"

"Now," Luke said. He cocked his head in the direction of the terrace, then started toward the doors. When he looked back, Colin had made his apologies to his friends and was following him.

The wind off the lake was frigid, so cold it sapped the breath from his lungs. But it did clear his head, and by the time Colin joined him, Luke was ready to get right to the point. "Why didn't you tell me?"

Colin frowned. "Tell you what?"

"About you and Maggie. Isabelle told me you're engaged."

A bland smile broke across Colin's face. "Yeah. Isn't it great? I asked and she said yes." His smile faded when Luke didn't return the good humor. "What? Was I supposed to ask your permission?"

"You could have told me."

"You're her friend, Fitzpatrick, not her father, and not even her brother. I don't need to ask your permission."

Luke cursed out loud. "What is this? I thought we were friends. I introduced you to Maggie. You know how close we are."

"Were," Colin corrected. "I wanted to tell you, but Maggie wanted to keep it a surprise."

"Do you love her?"

"What kind of question is that? Of course I love her."

"You're sure?"

Colin sighed and leaned back on the terrace railing. "As sure as a guy like me can be. Our relationship isn't perfect, but whose is? We care about each other, we never argue and we want the same things out of life— a home and a family."

"Do you want that? Or are you simply trying to please your father?"

"Ah," Colin said, laughing dryly. "I see what this is all about. You're questioning my motives. Well, you can go to hell, Fitzpatrick. I'm going to marry Maggie and we're going to be happy. And I'm also going to be named president of Spencer Enterprises. If you'll excuse me, I've got to see to my guests."

With that, Colin turned on his heel and walked back inside. Luke stood on the terrace for a long time, watching his friend through the windows. The man had a cocky arrogance that suddenly rubbed Luke the wrong way. A gust buffeted the terrace and Luke shoved his hands in his jacket pockets and turned his face into the wind.

This was none of his business. He'd already pressed the matter with Colin and tested the strength of their friendship. He wasn't willing to risk his bond with Maggie. If she'd agreed to marry Colin, he'd have to support her decision, without any interference.

Luke slowly crossed the terrace and opened the door. The sound of the music and the crowd drifted out into the cold. Hell, wasn't this what he wanted? He'd taken responsibility for Maggie so long ago, watching over her, worrying about her. Now someone else would take over and he could get on with his life. He could focus on his work without an ounce of guilt or remorse.

And he'd start right away. He'd leave this stuffy celebration and get back to what he did best. There was a military action waiting for him and he had a good eight hours before he had to be in the air and on his way to Albania. The time could be put to better use than guzzling champagne and singing "Auld Lang Syne" with a snooty crowd of Chicago bluebloods.

As for Maggie, she could make her announcement without him. After all, she no longer considered him an important part of her life, why should it matter if he was in attendance? As Luke wove through the guests on his way to the door, he couldn't deny he'd been the cause of this, that it was his fault Colin was in Maggie's life.

But it wasn't only regret that tore at him and pricked his anger. It was something more, something he wasn't at all expecting. He was jealous. Now the only thing he needed to figure out was why.

2

MAGGIE STOOD in the high-tech kitchen of Colin's apartment, three floors below the reception hall, a carton of Häagen-Dazs in her hand. She scooped out a glob of butter pecan and licked it off the spoon, staring distractedly at her reflection in the polished refrigerator door. She should look happy, luminous, like a bride-to-be. Isn't that how a woman was supposed to look when she'd found the man of her dreams?

Maybe it was just the refrigerator, she mused. She never looked good in stainless steel. She set the ice cream down and grabbed a towel, then began to polish the refrigerator door. There really wasn't any reason to be nervous. After careful consideration, Colin Spencer met all the criteria on her list. He fit right into her plan. What more did she want?

Maggie was never without a plan. Her first had been the "high school" plan—to graduate from Potter's Junction High with straight A's. Immediately after the ceremony, she'd put her "escape" plan into action—leaving Potter's Junction without looking back. Then there had been the "college" plan and the "career" plan. Her "marriage" plan, the most elaborate of all, had included a detailed outline of what she wanted in a husband—and Colin fit her requirements perfectly.

Planning every step of her life had been the only way to cope with an unpredictable childhood. Living with her mother, the queen of marital misfortune, Maggie had to find something to depend on. How many times had she tried to protect her mother from her runaway passions? With every new man, Maggie had offered sage advice and careful criticism, outlining the guy's faults in logical order. But her mother had no use for logic. Love was all that mattered. Unfortunately, love never seemed to last for Marlene Kelley.

That wouldn't be the way it was for her daughter, because Maggie had her plan. She'd written it down long ago, right after she'd graduated from college. It began with all the qualities she wanted in a husband then moved on to acceptable professions and ideal physical attributes. She'd even decided what kind of family she wanted as her in-laws.

By the time she'd met Colin, she'd nearly decided to rewrite the plan. Though she hadn't dated a lot of men, none of them had even come close to measuring up. But as she got to know Colin, she slowly began to realize this was a man she could marry. One by one, she had ticked off the entries on her list until there were only a few points left.

"Passion," she murmured. She stepped back from the refrigerator and stared at her reflection again.

Maybe she'd been a little too optimistic on that point. After all, wild and sweaty sex wasn't that important. And all the books and magazines claimed that passion mellowed as the marriage went on, that affection and respect were much more crucial than uncontrollable lust.

But it would have been nice to start with wild need and uninhibited desire rather than lukewarm enthusiasm. Maggie felt a warm blush work its way up her cheeks. She couldn't imagine Colin letting his libido overcome his customary composure. He was so polite, so proper when it came to bedroom etiquette. Maggie suspected it was all in the way he was raised. Eunice and Edward hadn't slept in the same room in years and they rarely showed any affection toward each other. No wonder Colin was so reserved.

In truth, Maggie was glad she wasn't driven by her desires and even happier that Colin wasn't, either. Desire could be nothing but trouble. It ruined relationships and was the root of all her mother's problems. No, Maggie could certainly live without desire.

She pushed the top back onto the ice-cream carton and put it back in the freezer, then slowly walked to the front door. As she grabbed the doorknob, a soft knock sounded on the other side.

When she pulled it open, she expected to see Colin waiting patiently near the elevator. Instead, Luke Fitzpatrick stood in the hallway, dressed in jeans and a battered leather jacket. Her pulse skipped and a smile touched her lips. She held out her hands and he took her fingers in his. Though they rarely saw each other lately, when they did, it seemed as if they'd never been apart. "You came," she said. "I wasn't sure you would."

"I wouldn't miss it."

She gave him a quick hug, then stepped back to look up at him. Lord, he was handsome. Even when they were kids, she had been acutely aware of the stares he'd drawn, the soft sighs and whispers from all the most popular girls at school. But he had never paid any notice to the others. When he was with Maggie, she was the only girl in the world, a Cinderella in a world of ugly stepsisters.

Even now, as he looked at her, Maggie knew Luke's attention was focused completely and irrevocably on her, if only for the next few minutes. Funny, but she'd never felt that way with Colin. They could spend a whole evening alone together and part of his mind was always occupied with business concerns.

"You look beautiful tonight," Luke said, giving her fingers a squeeze.

Maggie loved the feel of his hands, so strong and sure. She remembered the very first time he'd held her hand. She'd been chased home from school by a neighborhood bully and had tripped and skinned her knee on the sidewalk. Luke had found her there, bloodied and weeping and cowering beneath the bully's threats. He'd pulled her to her feet, dusted her off and promptly punched the bully square in the stomach. From that moment on, he'd been her hero.

"And you obviously didn't read your invitation," she murmured, reaching up to brush his hair off his forehead. It was a gesture so benign and offhand, she barely thought about it. But as the strands slipped through her fingers, so thick and soft, her gaze met his and held. A slow tingle numbed her fingers and she frowned, then pulled her hand away, confused by the odd sensation.

"I didn't have time to change," Luke said. "I'm sorry. I would have rented a monkey suit, but—"

She dragged her eyes away from his handsome face, realizing she was staring. "Well, I can fix that," Maggie said, grabbing his hand and pulling him inside. "Colin has a closet full of formal wear. I'm sure he has something to fit you."

Luke shook his head. "I'm not sure Colin would want—"

"Colin would want whatever makes me happy," Maggie replied. "And right now, I'd love to see my friend, Luke Fitzpatrick, in a tux. Come on, the millennium only comes around once every thousand years. Live a little."

She dragged a reluctant Luke to the bedroom. Maggie went over to Colin's closet, threw open the doors and studied the selection. She'd become accustomed to her fiancé's penchant for business suits, but when Luke gasped, she glanced over her shoulder and smiled. "I know. How can one guy wear all these? But he does," Maggie assured him. "I think Colin came out of the womb in a suit and tie."

When she found his tuxedos, Maggie grabbed one at random, and snatched a freshly laundered pleated shirt from another row of hangers. She pushed them both at Luke, then went to Colin's dresser and found a set of studs, cuff links and a bow tie. "Would it be too much to ask that you wear the same shoe size as Colin?" she said, staring down at his feet.

"Nine and a half," Luke said.

"Ten," she replied cheerfully, reaching for a pair of black leather evening shoes. "If you put on extra socks they should fit. Colin keeps his socks in the top drawer. The black ones are always on the right."

"Maggie, I don't think Colin would—"

"Forget about Colin," she said. "Just get dressed." With that, Maggie turned and walked out of the room, pulling the door shut behind her. She strolled into the living room and walked over to the wide wall of windows that overlooked the city.

She wasn't sure how long she stood there, staring out at nothing, an image of Luke's smile drifting through her mind. But when she heard him call her name, she turned around. Luke stood near the sofa, his fingers working at a stud, his shirt open to the waist. Maggie swallowed hard, then blinked, her eyes drawn to the smooth expanse of his muscular chest.

"Why don't they just put buttons on these shirts?

How's a guy supposed to get these little things through the holes?''

Maggie cleared her throat, frozen in place in front of the windows. She'd seen Luke without a shirt any number of times. Why did it bother her so much now? "You—you just push it through the...and then there's a little...it's really quite simple if you..."

With a frustrated sigh, Luke crossed the room and stood in front of her. He grabbed her hand and dropped the studs into her palm. "You do it, or we'll be here all night."

Oddly enough, Maggie found the prospect intriguing. Suddenly, she didn't want to go back upstairs. Her nerves were on edge and she felt a queasiness in her stomach. And on top of that, her hands were trembling and she couldn't seem to think straight.

She took a stud and carefully pushed it through the crisp fabric of his shirt. When her fingers grazed warm skin, she jumped as if she'd been burned and the studs scattered over the parquet floor. With a soft cry, Maggie dropped to her knees and frantically tried to gather them up. But her fingers had inexplicably gone numb.

Luke bent down beside her and picked the studs off the floor, then pulled her up with him. "Are you all right?" he asked, gazing into her eyes.

"I'm fine," Maggie replied, her voice cracking slightly.

What was wrong with her? She felt all jittery, her heart pounding in her chest and her pulse racing, as if she'd had too much caffeine. There wasn't caffeine in champagne, was there?

"Are you nervous about the announcement?" Luke asked, studying her shrewdly as he worked on the studs.

Her gaze drifted down his chest, following a thin

line of dark hair. When her eyes reached his waistband, she moved to an idle contemplation of his belly,
so flat and hard.

"Maggie?"

Startled, she looked up at him. This time, the flush
went from her chest up to her cheeks. "I—I'm sorry.
What were you saying?"

"Maggie, I know about the announcement. Your engagement. You seem a little nervous."

"My engagement?"

"Isabelle told me you and Colin are engaged."

Drawing in a sharp breath, she glanced at her left
hand, then held it out. "Yes. We are," she murmured,
forcing a bright smile. "We are engaged. See?"

When she risked another glance up, she noticed he'd
managed to fasten two of the studs, effectively hiding
his chest from view. But his chest wasn't her concern
anymore. Instead, she was worried about the probing
look in his pale blue eyes, eyes that had always been
able to see right into her soul.

"Do you love him?" Luke asked, his expression direct and unyielding.

"Who?" Maggie swallowed, then realized what he'd
asked. "Oh, Colin. Of course I do. I'm marrying him,
aren't I?"

Good grief, why couldn't she think? Her mind was
whirling with bizarre images and unbidden thoughts.
She took a long, deep breath and tried to focus, but all
that came into her head was the memory of how warm
and smooth Luke's skin had been. How much champagne had she drunk? She could only remember two
glasses, but she felt as if she'd guzzled an entire bottle.

He nodded. "I want you to be happy, Maggie. That's
all I care about. Are you happy?"

Maggie nodded, her head bobbing up and down uncontrollably. She ran her hand along her neck and pushed her thumb under her chin to stop it, but her brain kept right on bouncing inside her head. "I am happy," she said. "Very happy."

"He's good to you, then?"

She drew another long breath. "And if he isn't, you'll come and punch him in the stomach, right?"

Her joke fell flat. Luke didn't even break a smile. Instead, he tucked his shirt into his pants, and pulled the bow tie out of his pants pocket, a grim expression on his handsome face.

"Really," Maggie said softly, taking the tie from his hands and draping it around the wing collar. "Colin is everything I've always wanted. He'll make a good husband."

Luke studied her for a long moment, then tipped his chin up and looked at the ceiling. "And if he doesn't, I *will* come and punch him out." When she'd fastened the tie, he returned his gaze to her face. "I never thought, when I introduced you two, it would end this way."

His words seemed tinged with regret. "How did you think it would end?" Maggie asked. "Did you think he'd break my heart?"

Luke shook his head. "No, I thought you might break his heart. In fact, I was counting on it."

Maggie blinked in surprise, before carefully straightening his tie and pulling her hands away. "Why?" He looked uneasy and attempted to shrug off her question, but Maggie continued to stare at him quizzically. What had he meant?

"From the moment I met Colin, I admired him," Luke finally said. "He managed to be a nice guy, even though he had everything I always thought I wanted—

money, prestige, power. But he didn't have you. I had sole possession of that pleasure."

"And now he does?"

"Yeah, the guy has all the luck." With a sheepish shrug, Luke held out his hands and made a slow turn. "So, how do I look?"

Maggie grabbed the tuxedo jacket from the back of the sofa and handed it to him. "You look… wonderful." He shrugged into the jacket and she couldn't help noticing his shoulders were broader than Colin's and his arms more muscular. "It fits pretty well," she said, smoothing her palms over the finely tailored lapels.

He reached down and captured her hands, pressing them flat against his chest. Maggie felt his heart beating beneath her fingertips, strong and sure. "I'm happy for you, Maggie. You have all my best wishes."

Right now, she didn't want his best wishes. She was more interested in running her hands along his torso, slowly tugging his shirt open until she could once again touch his skin. "Thank you," she murmured in a strangled voice. "Now why don't you head back upstairs. I've got a few more things I need to do down here."

"I'll wait and walk you up," he insisted.

Maggie shook her head, once again desperate to be alone, to put aside these silly feelings. "No, go up and tell Colin I'll be there in a few minutes. He's probably wondering where I am. He hates it when I'm late."

With a resigned grin, Luke turned toward the door. Before he got there, he stopped and glanced back at her. "You're sure about this? About marrying Spencer?"

Maggie sent him a bright smile. "I'm sure."

By the time Luke closed the door behind him, Maggie wasn't sure of anything. She sat down on the sofa and stared down at her hands clasped in front of her. The diamond twinkled in the low light of the apartment. She twisted it around her finger, working it up toward her knuckle. "I'm just a little nervous," she murmured in an attempt to reassure herself.

But could she explain away the feelings that had raced through her just moments before to a simple case of nerves? Or was it something entirely different?

LUKE STEPPED into the elevator and leaned against the rear wall. He drew a long breath, then let it out slowly. What the hell was going on with him? He rubbed at his chest with his fingers, trying to brush away the warm brand left by Maggie's fleeting touch.

From the moment he walked in the door of Colin's apartment, something had been different. He usually felt so comfortable around Maggie. Tonight, he couldn't seem to relax. With every touch of her fingers, his heart raced, and with every word she said, he found himself searching for hidden meanings, evaluating the truth in her tone.

In the end, he could find nothing that would make him question her decision to marry Colin Spencer. She seemed content, almost serene, as if she were in the midst of a pleasant dream he'd intruded upon.

Her image drifted into his mind and he sighed. Lord, she was beautiful. He'd never really noticed before, her appearance was something he'd taken for granted for so long. But Maggie Kelley possessed a beauty unlike any other woman he'd ever known, an inner beauty that radiated outward until every one of her delicate features bordered on sheer perfection.

As a little girl, she'd been so skinny and frail. Her pale hair and complexion caused her to fade in the presence of prettier girls. As she'd grown, she'd changed, so slowly he'd barely noticed. Looks that had once seemed unremarkable had transformed into a gentle beauty that was undeniably compelling.

Even now, he could picture the incredible green of her eyes and the perfection of her lips. Her skin was nearly flawless and her pale hair was like spun flax. He'd always accepted her appearance in a casual, almost offhand manner. He frowned. Since when had her beauty become so tantalizing? So irresistible?

"Since she decided to marry another man," Luke muttered to himself. That's what this was all about. Maggie was suddenly more attractive to him because someone else wanted her. He'd done the same thing with an old bike he'd fixed up as a kid. For a long time, he'd considered it nothing more than a piece of junk. But then his grandmother had given it to one of the neighbor kids. Suddenly, he'd wanted that old bike more than a brand-new shiny one.

Luke shook his head. Maggie wasn't an old bike. She was someone he valued above anyone else in his life. And he couldn't help feeling as if he'd lost her to a rival. Was his reaction just a result of a bruised ego? Or did he have deeper feelings for Maggie that had only surfaced just now?

"Right," Luke muttered. "And what can you offer her that Colin can't?"

In truth, she belonged with a guy like Spencer. He could provide everything she'd ever need in life. He had a job that kept him in the city, he made great money and he never had to worry about job security—his last name assured him of that. And as much as Luke wanted to believe Spencer was a self-centered jerk, he knew Colin would be good to Maggie. Underneath his studied arrogance, Spencer was a pretty nice guy at heart.

Then why was Luke so tempted to throw a wrench into this engagement? Why did he want to destroy Maggie's first and only chance at happiness? Maybe *he* was the self-centered jerk instead of Colin. Maybe his own arrogance had caused him to believe he could get anything he wanted, through sheer will. After all, that's how he'd made his own successes. He'd ignored the dangers and the pitfalls and set his sights on a goal, never stopping until he'd achieved it, no matter who he pushed aside along the way.

And what would he do with Maggie if he had her? Luke had never wanted a permanent relationship. There were certainly plenty of other women who had offered. But his job was the most important thing in his life, more important than love and commitment. He'd made his choices and there was no point in wanting something he could never have—even if what he wanted at this moment was Maggie Kelley.

The elevator doors opened on the top floor of the Spencer Center and Luke stepped out. The tuxedo didn't make him feel any more comfortable than his regular attire, but he could certainly move through the crowd without causing any comments or curious looks. He caught sight of Colin, and decided apologies were in order.

As he approached, his buddy watched him with a wary eye. Colin made his excuses to the people he was with and started toward Luke. They met in the middle of the ballroom. Colin's gaze took in the change of clothes.

"Is that my Armani?"

Luke winced. "I'm sorry. Maggie insisted and, as you know, she's hard to refuse." He cleared his throat.

"And as long as I'm making apologies, I'm sorry for jumping on your case earlier. I shouldn't have—"

Colin held up his hand. "I wouldn't have expected anything less. I know you had Maggie's best interests at heart."

"Still, it's none of my business what goes on between you two. If she wants to marry you, I'm all right with that." But as he said the words, he knew they were a lie. He wasn't even close to all right.

"I'm glad you see that," Colin said, an uneasy expression crossing his face. "And I guess, maybe your instincts were partially right. I mean, my father does have something to do with my decision to get married. But that doesn't change how I feel about Maggie."

"What are you saying?"

Colin shrugged. "I'm saying if I wasn't getting pressure from the family, I might have waited a little longer. I mean, I know I want to marry Maggie, eventually. But I guess there will always be this little part of me that wonders what might have happened if I weren't a Spencer."

"This is no time for doubts," Luke warned.

Colin chuckled. "Hey, what guy doesn't have a few doubts? If every man who had doubts balked at getting married, this world would be filled with happy bachelors and frustrated spinsters."

Luke couldn't disagree with Colin. After all, marriage was a big step. And it was part of the male psyche to resist the pull of commitment until the very end. But this was *his* Maggie they were talking about. And she had chosen a guy who wasn't absolutely, positively certain about marriage. Maggie deserved to know this, didn't she?

His friend looked around the ballroom, his gaze

skimming over the crowd. "I still haven't seen Maggie. Didn't she come up with you?"

Luke shook his head. "No. She's still downstairs." And he intended to go right back down and find her.

Colin looked at his watch and grimaced. "Actually, I've got to go talk to our bankers. We're right in the middle of a deal and I've got a few kinks I need to discuss with them. Would you mind rounding her up? We're supposed to meet my parents up at the bandstand about ten minutes before midnight."

That Colin couldn't spare a few minutes to escort his fiancé into the party proved his point. Luke tried to tell himself it was none of his business, but old habits died hard.

Though Maggie was an adult, twenty-nine years old, he didn't want to believe she could make her own decisions about her future, not when it came to marrying a guy like Colin. "Maybe it's time she heard your opinion," Luke muttered, heading back to the elevator.

He waited at the elevator doors for a long time and, after five minutes, he decided to take the stairs. He jogged down two flights, but when he turned the corner for the forty-eighth floor, he noticed a shadow on the stairs. A few steps more and he realized Maggie was sitting on the bottom step. She sat silently, her hands folded in her lap, her gaze fixed on the toes of her shoes.

Luke paused and then took the last few steps slowly. "Maggie?"

Startled, she turned to look over her shoulder at him. "Hi," she said in a tiny voice.

"Maggie, they're waiting for you upstairs. Colin sent me to find you. What are you doing here?"

"Hmm," she said. "There's something wrong with the elevators."

"You could take the stairs," he suggested.

"Oh, thanks," she said. "But I'll wait a few more minutes."

He studied her for a long moment, then sat down beside her. Was she having second thoughts? She didn't seem anxious to rejoin her fiancé. "What's wrong? Why are you still hiding out down here?"

"I was just thinking," she said.

"About what?"

"About how things could have been so different, so awful. I mean, look at where I came from, what my mother was like. It could have all turned out so differently." She looked at him, her green eyes wide. "If it hadn't been for you."

"I didn't have that much to do with it. You would have turned out pretty wonderful even if I wasn't there."

She shook her head. "No, I don't think so." Maggie returned to a contemplation of her shoes. "Do you think I'll make a good wife?"

Luke slipped his arm around her shoulders and she leaned into him. The sweet scent of her hair touched his nose and he fought an urge to draw her even closer, to pull her body against his, to make her forget about Colin. "I think you will."

"Because I don't want to mess it up like my mother did. What if it's genetic?"

He chuckled. "I've never heard of a divorce gene, Maggie. If you marry a man who loves you, then you won't mess up. Trust me." His mind raced as he tried to come up with the words to convince her that Colin Spencer was that man. But his talent with language deserted him and every thought seemed selfish and petty.

Maggie drew a ragged breath then let it out slowly. "All right. I'm ready. Let's go."

Luke helped Maggie to her feet, then slipped her hand into the crook of his elbow. One step at a time, they began to climb the stairs. But with each flight of stairs, Luke's frustration grew. Why couldn't he tell her how he felt? Why couldn't he warn her against marrying Colin?

"If you have any doubts, we can turn around and walk right back down," he ventured. As soon as the words left his lips, he regretted saying them. Maggie wasn't the one with doubts. He was!

"I don't have any doubts. I've thought about this very carefully," Maggie said.

When they reached the fifty-first floor, he paused, his hand on the doorknob, tempted to grab her arm and keep her trapped in his embrace until after midnight. He turned his options over and over in his head, trying to find the right course.

Sure, he might be able to convince Maggie not to marry Colin, but what then? Was he prepared to offer her something better? It would take a hell of a lot to top what Colin Spencer could give her. And Luke certainly didn't have marriage in mind. At least Spencer was willing to lay it all out there, to marry Maggie and vow to take care of her. Luke wasn't prepared to offer her much more than a shoulder to cry on.

With a silent curse, he yanked open the door and gently steered her through it. How could he convince her? When the clock struck midnight and the new millennium began, their lives were destined to take separate paths and their friendship would be changed forever. But there had to be a way to change destiny. He'd just have to figure it out in the next few minutes.

MAGGIE STEPPED through the door to the lobby of the reception hall. The sound of the band drifted into the hallway and, for a moment, she hesitated. Colin would be waiting, along with his parents and the four hundred assorted guests and business associates.

Luke squeezed her hand. "There's still time to change your mind," he said. "We can turn around and walk away."

Maggie turned to smile at his teasing, but Luke's expression was dead serious. For a fleeting moment, she wanted to take his hand and run for the stairs, to escape the little doubts that pricked at her mind. What if she was settling for less than she deserved, as Isabelle had said? What if there was a man out there who could love her, passionately and completely? Her heart stopped for a moment. Oh, Lord, what if that man was Luke? "Don't be silly," she said in a stiff voice.

"Are you sure you're all right?" Luke asked.

Maggie nodded. "I'm fine. Let's go."

As they walked into the reception area, Maggie's grip tightened on Luke's fingers. She took a deep breath and pasted a smile on her face when she saw Eunice and Edward Spencer standing near the bandstand. Her gaze searched for Colin, but he was nowhere to be seen. Where was he? It wasn't like Colin to be late, especially for something so important.

When Eunice saw them both, she hurried up to Maggie and grabbed her hands, drawing her away from Luke, away from safety. "Where's Colin?" she whispered.

Maggie blinked in surprise. "I—I don't know. He should be here somewhere. I haven't seen him since earlier this evening. He probably got caught up with some of his business associates."

"We have to make the announcement right before

midnight," Eunice said, an hysterical note creeping into her voice. "Otherwise, it just won't be special. It has to be special to rate a mention in the society pages. And we can't make the announcement without Colin."

"He'll be here," Maggie said calmly. "We still have five minutes."

She took her place near the corner of the bandstand, flanked by Eunice and Edward. They all stared silently at the revelers, waiting for the moment before the countdown began.

"Maybe he's become ill," Eunice said, glancing past Maggie to her husband. "He wasn't looking very well the last time I saw him. And there is that flu going around."

Edward stood stiffly, his hands folded in front of him. He always looked as if he'd just finished sucking a big bag of lemons, Maggie mused.

"Or maybe he's contracted a case of cold feet," Edward muttered. "That boy will shame this family, mark my words. This isn't the first time he's backed out on a marriage proposal."

Maggie gasped, her eyes widening. "What?"

Eunice grabbed her hand and patted it sympathetically. "Don't listen to him, dear. He's never been a patient man. It's just water."

"Water?" Maggie asked.

"Under the bridge, dear," Eunice added with a sniff.

"You mean Colin's done this before?"

"It was a long, long time ago," she explained, "and he was very young. He wasn't ready for marriage. And the girl, well, she was—a sow's ear."

Maggie frowned. Did Eunice Spencer always speak in old adages? She'd never noticed before. "A sow's ear?"

"You know, silk purse, sow's ear. She was the ear."

"What about that girl he met after graduate school?" Edward asked with a snort. "He dumped her without a look back and her family had millions. And then there was that Carla or Darla or—"

"Sharla," Eunice corrected, turning to Maggie. "Another ear. And they were never engaged anyway."

Edward raised a bushy white eyebrow. "She said there were promises made. And we paid dearly for those promises."

"How—how many other women have there been?" Maggie asked, stunned by these sudden revelations.

"Not many," Eunice said. "And he never loved them the way he loves you, dear. There has to be a reason he's late. Maybe he's been kidnapped. Or it could be…food poisoning! Those shrimp didn't smell right to me."

"Don't be absurd, Eunice. The boy has shirked his family responsibilities again. When it comes to women, he's an idiot. I blame you for this, Eunice. You coddle him."

Eunice puffed out her ample chest and huffed disdainfully. "Me? Me?" she accused, keeping her voice under control and out of range of the guests. "I can't control the boy. He's your son. You know, he could be in the men's room. Go look, Edward."

Maggie's stomach churned and she tried to maintain her composure. Was this as horrible as it seemed? Or was she just numb from nerves? Eunice and Edward actually believed Colin had run out on her. How could that be? He cared about her, he wanted to marry her. And what about these other women? Why hadn't he ever mentioned the other women? She searched the crowd, but not for Colin. She wanted Luke. He'd make everything right.

The bandleader stepped over to Edward and

pointed to his watch, a look of grave concern on his face. Colin's father gave the man an irritated shrug, then turned his gaze back toward the doors. "He's not coming," Edward muttered.

"He'll be here," Eunice said.

"Ladies and gentlemen, it's time to start the countdown to the millennium!" The bandleader's voice echoed through the hall and Maggie winced at the strident sound. As he began the countdown, her ears filled with a low roar and her body felt weightless. It seemed like everyone in the crowd watched them, standing at the corner of the stage with nothing at all to announce. Maggie wondered if her smile looked as fake as it felt, if her eyes betrayed her utter humiliation.

"Ten, nine, eight…"

He wasn't coming. It was obvious to Maggie that Colin had had second thoughts. There would be no announcement. Perhaps no engagement. She twisted the diamond on her finger, tempted to tear it off and throw it into the crowd.

"Seven, six, five…"

How could she have been so stupid? She'd trusted Colin. She'd invested her entire future in him. What was she supposed to do now? Time seemed to grind to a halt and the countdown slowed to an excruciating pace.

"Four…three…"

Maggie raised her eyes to the guests and, in the midst of the crowd, her gaze met Luke's. He stood surrounded by revelers, staring at her, as if his eyes could draw away some of the pain she felt. As if in slow motion, he took a step toward her, and then another and another, his hand outstretched.

"Two…"

He smiled at her, his expression filled with sympathy, and tears pushed at the corners of Maggie's eyes.

"One."

With a soft sigh, she crumpled into his embrace. His arms enfolded her and he pressed her face against the soft fabric of his jacket, stroking her hair and murmuring words of encouragement to her. A tiny sob escaped her throat and it was like all the years had melted away. She was back on that sidewalk, her knees skinned and her pride bruised. And her white knight had stepped out of the shadows to save her, once again.

"Happy New Year! And welcome to the new millennium!"

3

A CHEER ERUPTED from the crowd and the band broke into "Auld Lang Syne." Party horns shrieked and whistles blew. Streamers and confetti and balloons poured over the guests as kisses and handshakes were exchanged. But Maggie barely noticed. Shielding her from curious onlookers, Luke wrapped his arm around her shoulders and led her toward the doors to the terrace. They stepped outside and he immediately slipped out of his jacket and draped it over her shoulders.

An explosion of color rained overhead as fireworks burst in the night sky from the North Avenue beach. Maggie leaned over the terrace railing and drew a ragged breath of frigid air. "Happy New Year," she murmured.

She stared at the brilliant display of light—purple and green and blue, like shooting stars tumbling into the lake. From the street, the sound of car horns drifted up on the icy winter wind. It seemed as if the whole world had stopped to take note of Maggie's humiliation.

Luke gently grasped her shoulders and let his palms slide down her arms. "God, Maggie, I'm so sorry. I never thought—"

"What are you sorry about?" she asked, brushing an errant tear from her cheek. "You didn't have anything to do with this."

He gently turned her to face him, and tipped her chin up, wiping a tear away with his thumb. "Maybe this is for the best. If the guy didn't want to—"

"Stop it!" Maggie cried, pulling out of his grasp. "You don't need to stand up for me anymore! I'm the one who agreed to marry him. I'm the one he walked away from." She pressed the heels of her hands into her temples and slowly shook her head. After the first shock of Colin's desertion had worn off, Maggie couldn't help seeing the absurdity in the situation. Such a practical approach to marriage and they hadn't even made it as far as the announcement!

An unbidden giggle worked its way through her throat and burst from her lips. "I should be happy! At least I found out he didn't want me before he married me—instead of *after*. Always the gentleman, that Colin Spencer."

"Why do you do that?" Luke demanded, a trace of anger in his voice. "Why do you make excuses for people who hurt you? You did that when you were a kid and you're doing it now. Just stop it."

"Did you know about the other women?" Maggie asked. "He was engaged before. More than once."

Luke blinked, clearly surprised by the revelation. "I knew there was a serious relationship right after we graduated from college, but he told me *she* broke up with *him*."

A shiver raced through Maggie's body and suddenly she felt a frantic need to get off the terrace and out of the building. "What am I going to do?" she asked, starting for the doors. "Am I supposed to wait and hope that he'll come to his senses? Or should I walk away? What's the proper etiquette when you've been dumped in front of four hundred people?"

"Maggie, no one knew the announcement was coming. You don't have to be embarrassed."

"Why would he do this? I mean, if he didn't want to get married, why buy this ridiculous diamond?" She tried to pull the ring off her finger, but it wouldn't budge. Frustrated, she yanked harder, until the pain in her finger caused her to curse out loud. The ring stayed where Colin had placed it on Christmas Eve. Tears spilled from the corners of her eyes and she buried her face in her hands.

Luke stepped in front of her and drew her into his arms. "He doesn't deserve you. If he really loved you, he'd have been there at midnight."

Maggie nuzzled her face against his shoulder. Eunice had certainly come up with some creative excuses. Kidnapping? Colin wasn't exactly the Lindbergh baby. And according to Edward, he probably wouldn't be too anxious to get his son back. How far down the list had she been as a candidate for wife? Fifth or sixth? A fresh flood of tears sprang from her eyes.

"It will be all right, sweetheart," Luke said in a soothing voice. "I'll make it all right." He tipped her face up and gently kissed the tears on her cheek.

But Maggie didn't want his sympathy. And she was too mortified to make excuses for Colin. She slowly pulled away from Luke's embrace. "I should go back inside."

"Here you are!"

They both turned as Eunice bustled onto the terrace. A luxurious mink coat was casually tossed over her gown and even in the brisk wind, her platinum-blond hair stayed perfectly coiffed. Two security guards followed in her wake. "I have no doubt that something has happened to Colin. We've gathered the security staff and set them on a search. And the police are on their way. Maggie, dear, we'll get to the bottom of this before you can shed another tear."

Eunice grabbed Maggie's arm and hustled her toward the door. "Mice and men," she muttered. "Best laid schemes."

Maggie turned to Luke, sending him a pleading glance, and he followed. The guests had grown so exuberant over Eunice's millennium light show that they barely paid notice to the security guards who walked briskly at Maggie's side. By the time Maggie and Luke had reached the elevator bays, Eunice had been lost to an endless string of guests extending their best wishes for a happy new year. Obviously, social obligations were more important than finding her son.

None of the elevators appeared to be moving and they had waited nearly ten minutes when a gray-haired maintenance man burst out of the stairwell door. His name, Irv, was emblazoned across a patch on his heaving chest. "It's that damn computer bug," he muttered between breaths. "Y2K, my butt. I remember when elevators used to be run by elevator operators. What was wrong with that? A man can do a job better than a computer any day. We've had to reset the whole program. We're damn lucky we've got a generator." He studied the panel with the rest of them. "The cars will respond in a moment."

Just as the maintenance man had promised, the lights soon began to move on the panel next to the doors. All of the cars slowly descended to the first floor, paused for a moment, then began to rise to the penthouse level. A moment later, the doors of all three elevators opened simultaneously in front of them.

"If Mr. Spencer is still in the building, we'll find him," the first security guard assured her. "We'll take your story down in the office, miss, and get right on the case."

Maggie blinked. "My story? What story?"

The second guard frowned. "You were the last person to see Mr. Spencer, weren't you?"

Maggie shook her head. "I've barely talked to him all evening. Do you think I had something to do with this? That I did something to make him leave?"

The guard frowned. "Well, I don't know. Mrs. Spencer thought—"

"Miss Kelley is—was—Colin Spencer's fiancée," Luke growled. "She doesn't know where he is, so leave her alone."

With that, Luke grabbed Maggie's hand and pulled her into the elevator. When the guards made to follow them, he held out his hand to stop them both. "Take another car," he muttered.

A long sigh slipped from Maggie's lips as soon as the doors closed and she sank against the back wall of the elevator. Her heel came to rest on an empty champagne bottle that rolled back and forth on the polished parquet. She bent down and picked it up. "At least someone had a happy new year," she said.

"You don't have to talk to these guys if you don't want to. You can just leave."

"They think I had something to do with Colin's disappearance," Maggie said. "Maybe I did. He decided he didn't want to marry me and he took off. It's as simple as that."

"Maggie, I—"

"But then Colin could be in trouble. He could be...stuck in one of the elevators. That's possible, isn't it?" A tiny glimmer of hope captured her emotions. "It could be. Do you think?"

Luke shrugged. "I suppose it might be possible."

"Yes," Maggie said softly. "Maybe we're just imagining the worst."

She stood silently at Luke's side, her mind spinning with possibilities and probabilities. What if Colin turned up with a plausible excuse for his absence? Everything could go ahead as they planned and it would be as if nothing had happened at all. But this tiny bump in the road to happily-ever-after had shaken her deeply.

And there was something else that she couldn't ignore any longer. Through the humiliation and the anger and the confusion, another feeling kept popping up. She'd first realized it in the milliseconds after the midnight hour struck, and then again when the security guard had spoken to her.

Relief. She felt relief. All the little doubts that had nagged at her mind since she'd agreed to Colin's proposal were still there. Only now they were intensified, blown up larger than life until she couldn't brush them aside any longer. In a secret corner of her heart, she was glad the announcement hadn't happened. It gave her time to think.

But think about what? If only she could look into Colin's eyes and ask him for the truth. Did he really want to marry her or was he simply pacifying his parents? Was she the one he wanted or just another in a long line of women? Did he really love her, or were his feelings as shaky as hers?

As the only son of Eunice and Edward Spencer, Colin was expected to grow up, get a college degree, then settle down and get married. Maggie knew this. From the moment he'd left college, his parents had been waiting for him to find a wife and to produce an heir. To Maggie, the notion had seemed a bit archaic, but then, she'd never really understood the ways of the incredibly wealthy.

In the Spencer family, responsibility took precedence over happiness, business over personal matters. Maggie had accepted the long hours at the office. She'd even learned to accept Colin's taciturn nature, a characteristic he'd inherited from his father. But she wasn't sure she could accept that she hadn't been Colin's first choice for a wife.

"If you want to, Maggie, we can leave. We can get out of this elevator and keep walking. You don't have to deal with this now."

Maggie glanced up at Luke, her gaze resting on his handsome face. A surge of emotion filled her heart. Always the hero. Suddenly, she wanted to step back into his embrace, to feel his arms around her and to take comfort in his warmth. She wanted to touch his face and run her fingers through his hair, turn her mouth up to his and—

Maggie gulped back her runaway thoughts. Oh, it had to be the champagne…or all the emotion roiling inside her. Her fiancé had just dumped her and she was fantasizing about another man! "I—I'm fine, Luke. But thank you. It's good to know I've got a white knight waiting in the wings."

The elevator bumped to a stop and the doors opened to the spacious lobby of the Spencer Center. Marble and smoked glass gleamed in the soft light and a huge Christmas tree soared to nearly the top of the streetside atrium, filling the air with a pungent pine smell. Their footsteps echoed through the silence as they headed toward the security desk. The guards weren't far behind them.

Maggie stopped in front of the tree and turned to

Luke. "You should go upstairs," she murmured. "Isabelle is probably wondering where you are."

"I want to stay with you," Luke insisted. "Isabelle will understand. And I've talked to Colin a couple of times this evening. Maybe I can help."

Maggie shook her head. "This will probably all be solved in a few minutes. And there's no reason to ruin Isabelle's evening. Please, go back to the party. I'll see you up there later. I promise."

For a moment, Maggie thought he would acquiesce. But then in one determined move, he took her face between his hands and brought his mouth down on hers. The kiss was fierce and filled with frustration, startling her with its intensity. As quickly as he'd pulled her toward him, he stepped away.

A soft oath escaped his lips. "He doesn't deserve you."

Maggie stared up at him, stunned speechless. The muted scent of his cologne touched her nose and her senses whirled. She'd always loved the way he smelled, like fresh air and high adventure, like— She swallowed hard. Words wouldn't come.

"Do what you have to do." He said. "I'll be here when you're done." Luke gave her a curt nod, then strode to the elevator. She had never needed him more than she did now and she was tempted to call him back, to throw herself into his arms and kiss him again. But kissing Luke had created a whole new set of problems—problems she'd have to deal with later. Maggie drew a ragged breath and gathered her resolve. First, she'd deal with Colin. Then she'd figure out what had possessed Luke.

The security guard at the desk jumped up as she and the two men approached. "I think we've found him! Look! Here he is!"

Maggie pressed her fingers to her lips. "He's under the desk?"

The guard flushed and shook his head. "No, miss. He's here, on the videotape."

She came around the corner of the desk and stared at the row of television screens. "Where?"

The guard pointed to the first screen and she watched as a slow-motion tape rolled forward. The camera was trained on the elevator doors in the lobby. Her breath caught in her throat as she watched Colin exit the elevator and head toward the side entrance. Her heart ground to a halt when she saw who he was with.

"Isabelle," she murmured.

"Is that her name?" the guard asked. "Isabelle what?"

"Channing. Isabelle Channing."

"Well, we've got another shot of them outside on the street. They took off in a limo, but I couldn't get the tag number. And there doesn't seem to be any force involved." He paused, then cleared his throat. "They did look a little...drunk. See here." He pressed his finger to the screen. "She's stumbling a bit. And he has trouble with the car door."

"I—I see," Maggie said, trying to breathe, yet failing miserably. She couldn't believe what she'd witnessed, but there was no other explanation for it. Her fiancé had run off with her best girlfriend! Her mind spun back to the conversation she'd had with Isabelle, to the negative reaction Is had had to the news of Maggie's engagement. Could Isabelle have been in love with Colin all along? Or was this just some impromptu act of passion on her part?

"My life has turned into a very bad talk show," Maggie murmured, turning away from the screen. Her head buzzed and her knees shook as she walked to the elevators. "Maybe this has all been a bad dream. I'll just go upstairs and lie down and when I wake up, everything will be back to normal."

No matter how much she wanted it to be so, Maggie knew that the dawn would bring changes she didn't want to face. For so long, she'd searched for something or someone to build her future upon and she thought she'd found it in Colin.

Now Colin had run off with Isabelle and the only thing on Maggie's mind was the kiss she'd shared with Luke. She'd thought her life would be settled in the new millennium. But midnight had passed and she'd found nothing but chaos.

THE NOISE ON THE STREET filled Maggie's ears and jangled her thoughts. Though the Spencer Center lobby was brightly lit, most of the buildings along a three-block stretch of Michigan Avenue had gone dark. The distant clamor of a burglar alarm blended with the honking of horns and the laughter of people. As predicted, the power grid in the city had faltered, leaving only the cars and taxis to light the street in front of her.

Maggie barely noticed the confusion all around her. Instead, her mind was occupied with all that had passed in the last hour. After kissing Luke and then watching her fiancé escape with her best friend, she'd made her way back to Colin's apartment, she'd gathered up a few of her things and stuffed them into a pair of shopping bags. Though she'd practically lived with Colin, it seemed wrong to stay in his apartment now. She'd go back to her little condo in Wicker Park. There, she could start to plan for her future—a future without a husband and family.

Every facet of her existence had become so entangled with Colin's that she wondered how she'd ever extricate herself from it. The car she usually drove belonged to her fiancé. The gown she was wearing had been charged on Colin's account at Bloomingdale's. And worst of all, she'd given up her lease on the flower shop on Clark Street in preparation to take over a small retail space off the lobby of the Spencer Center—space that was managed by Colin himself.

Maggie bit her bottom lip and fought back a fresh round of tears. In a few months, she wouldn't even have a place to work. She'd have no way to make a living. How could things have gone so bad so quickly? Her life was a mess and she didn't know how to begin fixing it. But maybe—

She pushed aside another current of hope. Why did she persist in believing that everything would turn out in the end, that this pain would fade into complacency and then forgiveness? She would see him again since there were financial matters to tend to. Maybe then they could work things out. But he'd run off with another woman!

Could she accept excuses and explanations and begin where they'd left off? Or was this the end, here, sitting on a hard marble bench in the cold wind of a black winter night? She watched as couples walked past, filled with too much champagne and reveling in the unbridled exhilaration of an event they'd never see again in their lifetime.

People laughed and kissed and danced in the darkened street, unconcerned about the lack of electricity. Taxis and cars joined in a chorus of horns and, somewhere up Michigan Avenue, a brass band played. Maggie tried to imagine what she might have been doing at this very minute had the evening gone as planned. Would she be dancing with Colin? Or would his friends surround them, offering congratulations and best wishes?

She shivered and rubbed her hands together. The icy wind felt good on her heated face, numbing her fingers through her gloves and her toes through the thin satin pumps she wore. Maggie stood and walked to the curb, then waved for a cab. The first taxi ignored her outstretched hand, as did the next eight that passed.

Maggie sighed and her breath clouded in front of her face. She could catch the train back to Wicker Park. But her shoes weren't made for trekking through snowbanks and dodging slushy puddles and she didn't want to ride the El in her evening gown. Besides, she was pretty sure the train ran on electricity and she wasn't willing to risk spending the night on a stalled train somewhere between here and home.

"Maggie?"

His voice, so familiar, was like a powerful tranquilizer, instantly slowing her pulse and calming her nerves. Maggie turned and looked up at Luke, a soft sigh escaping her lips. His hands were jammed in his pants pockets and he had turned up the collar of Colin's tux against the cold. And he still looked devastatingly handsome, so handsome that she caught herself holding her breath. He glanced up and down Michigan Avenue. "The power's out?"

She nodded. "It went off about ten minutes ago."

"What are you doing out here in the cold?" he asked. "I stopped at Colin's apartment to find you, but you weren't there."

"I—I couldn't stay. I need to go home to my own place. I need to go somewhere where I can deal with this." She pointed to her shopping bags. "I've got your clothes. I was going to drop them at your office."

"I take it you never found Colin."

She shook her head and wrapped her arms around herself to still the tremors that rocked her body. "No," she murmured. She could handle the humiliation alone. But telling Luke made it more acute.

He nodded. "I went upstairs to find Isabelle, but she wasn't up there. I can't imagine how I could have missed her. She's probably mad as hell since I all but deserted her. But I guess she's a big girl, she can find her own way home."

"I think she already has." Maggie swallowed convulsively and considered her next words carefully. "She—she left with Colin. The security cameras caught them together. I saw them, on the videotape at the security desk."

Luke scowled, then furrowed his fingers through his hair. "Isabelle is the cause of all this trouble? My Isabelle?"

"I'd venture to guess that you're not going to be too quick to claim her anymore. The way it looked, she's Colin's Isabelle now."

Luke cursed out loud and began to pace the sidewalk in front of Maggie. "She's done a lot of outrageous things, but this takes the prize. Good God, Maggie, she knew how you felt about Colin. She knew about the engagement! How could she do something so heartless?"

In truth, Isabelle did know how Maggie felt about Colin. Her friend had seen through those lackluster declarations of love as if Maggie had been transparent as glass. Maybe Isabelle had even saved Maggie from the inevitable—a painful and messy breakup or a loveless marriage. Or even a divorce.

"I—I don't know. And frankly, I don't care. I'd just like to get a cab and get home."

He reached down and took her hands and rubbed

them between his. Maggie stared at his fingers, so strong and capable. He had beautiful hands and she slowly twisted her gloved fingers between his, amazed that simply touching him could make her feel so much better.

"Come on," Luke said. "My truck's parked in a lot down the street. I'll drive you home before you turn into a Popsicle."

Maggie nodded, grateful that he'd rescued her for a second time that night. "I'll go if you promise me one thing."

"Anything," he said.

"Let's not talk about what happened. I just can't think about this anymore. I'm sure I'll have to think about it again soon, but right now, I don't want to remember this night as something awful." She grabbed his arm and leaned into his body. "Everyone in the world will remember where they were at midnight on the millennium. They'll probably even remember who they were with, the song that was playing in the background, what they were wearing. I'd rather remember you driving me home than everything that happened upstairs."

As they strolled silently down Michigan Avenue, the power suddenly came back on, casting the sidewalk in the magical glow created by thousands of tiny white lights draped in the trees that lined the sidewalks. Maggie's breath caught as elaborate Christmas decorations flickered to life and stood in colorful contrast to the snow that swirled around them. The moment was filled with magic and she stopped and watched as one by one, the streetlights sputtered to life.

She glanced over at Luke, only to find him staring at her. For a heartbeat, their gazes locked and every thought of Colin slipped from her mind. Instead, her thoughts were occupied with the man beside her, the man who had come to her rescue once again, the man who had kissed her in the lobby. Snowflakes caught on his thick lashes and the wind ruffled his dark hair and she couldn't seem to take her eyes off him.

She fought the temptation to push up on her toes and kiss him again. A quick peck on the cheek, a thank-you for all he had done for her. In truth, though, Maggie wasn't interested in platonic gratitude. Her gaze drifted down to his finely sculpted lips and she wondered what might happen if she just brushed her mouth against his, lingered for a long moment. Would this spark of attraction she felt toward him burst into full-fledged desire? Would he kiss her again like he had in the lobby? Or was this strange fascination with his lips only an irrational way of coping with Colin's desertion.

"Maggie?"

She blinked then forced a smile. "What? Oh, right. Let's go. I'm—I'm cold."

By the time they pulled up at her coach house in Luke's Blazer, Maggie could almost breathe again. She'd kept her eyes fixed on the street in front of them for nearly the entire ride home, worried that if she looked at Luke again she'd slip into another irrational fantasy. Hero worship, that was all it was. He'd rescued her from a humiliating situation and her gratitude had somehow warped into an odd sexual attraction.

Luke hopped out of the truck and ran around to her side, then helped her out. She fumbled through her purse for her keys as they walked along the narrow passageway to the back of the property. The porch lights burned bright and Maggie unlocked the front door before turning back to him. She wanted to ask him in, to thank him once more for his kindness, but she was so cold her bones ached and so weary she couldn't think straight.

"Would you like me to come in?" he asked.

Maggie shook her head. "I'll be all right," she murmured, glancing up at him in the harsh glare. "Isabelle said—" She paused, purging the name from her thoughts. "So, you're leaving on an assignment tomorrow."

Luke nodded. "Albania. There's an uprising brewing and I'm covering it for the syndicate. I've got an interview with the leader of the rebel faction."

Maggie reached up and placed her palm on his cheek, staring into the face that had grown so handsome over the years. She could still see the boy there, in his easy smile and pale blue eyes, the way his thick, dark hair fell over his forehead in a careless wave. "Keep your head down, okay? And don't go playing the hero, even though you do it so well."

He bent closer and pressed his lips to her forehead. "You sure you'll be all right?"

Maggie nodded, then without a second thought, touched his lips with a quick kiss. She'd kissed him that same way so many times, for so many benign reasons. But this time, it was different. This time, she didn't want to step back. His breath was so warm against her cheek and the scent of his cologne teased at her nose. She could feel his strength seeping into her body just by standing close to him.

Their gazes locked and for a fleeting moment, she thought she saw desire flickering in his eyes. Against all common sense, she kissed him again, letting her lips linger a moment longer. When she pulled back this time, the expression on his face made her flush with embarrassment. He looked stunned, uneasy, as if he regretted what had just passed between them.

"Oh, God, I—I'm sorry," Maggie stammered, pressing her fingers to her damp lips. "I—I didn't mean to—I'm just so—"

But she never completed her explanation, for a moment later, Luke's mouth came down on hers, hard and firm, in a deep, soul-shattering kiss. His tongue teased at hers and she responded beneath him. Her fingers trembled and Maggie slid her palms up his lapels and twisted her hands through the hair at his nape.

The kiss turned frantic as Luke pulled her hard against his body and pressed her against the door. His hands slipped into her open coat and spanned her waist, his fingers digging into her flesh until she thought she might cry out. A flood of desire coursed through her veins and, suddenly, she wasn't cold anymore.

Then, as abruptly as it began, the kiss ended. Luke pulled back and shoved his hands in his pockets, cursing softly beneath his breath and shaking his head. "I—it's late. I gotta go." He frowned at her, then turned away. A moment later, he looked back. "We shouldn't have done that."

An anxious smile twitched at her lips and she could feel the heat ebb from her flushed cheeks. "We've both had too much champagne," she said, knowing that she'd barely touched a glass at the party.

"Right. Too much champagne," he agreed, though Maggie suspected he'd had very little to drink as well. He seemed in complete control of himself, beyond his ragged breathing and the hard set of his jaw.

But there had to be an excuse for what had just happened between them! Luke was her friend, a man who had been like a big brother to her. She'd never considered him anything more. Yet, she wanted him to draw her into his arms again, to feel his strong hands caressing her body, his warm tongue tracing her lower lip and delving into her mouth.

She swallowed convulsively, then slowly reached back for the door. "I—I'd better go in now."

"I think that would be best," he said, his eyes still fixed on hers.

"Thanks for the ride," she murmured, turning the knob and pushing the door open behind her. "Call me when you get back, all right?"

Luke reached out as if to touch her again, then thought better of it and pulled his hand back. "You take care of yourself, Maggie. I hope that—" He paused and reconsidered what he was about to say. "Things will look better in the morning. I promise." With that, he turned and bounded down the porch steps, disappearing into the dark shadows between the house and the street.

With a soft sigh, Maggie picked up the shopping bags, stepped inside and closed the door behind her. She leaned back against the door and slid to the floor, clutching her knees in front of her. Her mind returned again and again to that instant on the porch when he'd kissed her, until all the feelings came flooding back, so deliciously intense.

She stared at the shopping bags, and realized that she'd forgotten to give Luke his clothes. Maggie grabbed the bags and dumped the contents out in front of her. Snatching up Luke's leather jacket, she pressed it against her face, inhaling the scent of leather and his cologne. Maggie closed her eyes, letting the smell soothe her nerves.

She had gained and lost a fiancé all in one week. She'd been humiliated in front of his parents and betrayed by a woman she'd trusted. Worse than all that, with just a stupid impulse, she'd risked a friendship that she valued over everything else in her life. Things would be forever changed between her and Luke, and all because of a stupid impulse, an ill-timed kiss.

Maggie put her fingers to her lips, trying to rub away the warm imprint of his mouth. Then she tipped her head back and looked at her palm. In the dim light, she could see the little star near the base of her thumb.

"The mark of the millennium," she murmured. "This is why I don't believe in fortune-tellers."

LUKE RUBBED his bloodshot eyes and squinted at the computer screen. No matter how hard he tried to concentrate on work, he couldn't seem to put Maggie out of his mind.

He had driven around the city for over two hours after he'd dropped her off, caught in the midst of traffic jams and sporadic power outages and crowds of revelers who still hadn't made their way home. When he had finally reached the Global Press Syndicate headquarters in the Loop, he'd grabbed his bags out of the back of the truck and headed up to his office. He'd changed out of Colin's tux and decided to get in a few more hours of research before he headed to O'Hare.

Luke wanted plenty of background material to study on the plane. There would be a long flight to Athens and then a couple of short hops to put him inside Albanian borders. After that, he'd have to rely on local transportation to reach rebel headquarters. He wasn't worried about that. He was more concerned with the time he'd spend in the air, the endless hours with nothing better to do than replay the kiss he'd shared with Maggie, over and over again.

Hell, how had he made such a mess of things? That

first kiss in the lobby at the Spencer building had been little more than sheer frustration mixed with too much champagne. But it had opened a door that until that moment, had been firmly closed, a door Maggie had shoved right open when she'd kissed him on her front steps.

That's the kiss he truly regretted, the one borne out of desire. He'd taken complete advantage of Maggie's situation—and her fragile emotional state. What kind of man was he that he'd deliberately risk a friendship more precious to him than his very life for a brief moment of passion? Maggie Kelley had been the only bright spot in a rocky adolescence and she still had the capacity to light up his life with just a simple smile.

Like Maggie, he'd lived in a single-parent household, but instead of a mother that preferred matrimony over child-rearing, Luke had been left with a grandmother who watched him like a hawk. He couldn't claim abuse or even neglect, though having a drunk for a father and a mother who disappeared when he was two certainly didn't make for a typical American family.

Though his grandmother had been a good parent, he'd never felt he could confide in her. Admitting he had problems would only cause her needless concern. But when he had found Maggie, cowering beneath a bully's fists, her knees bloodied and her pretty face streaked with tears, he'd found a true friend.

She was three years younger than he was, so there had never been any romantic feelings to get in the way. When he became a teenager, she was still playing with dolls. And when he'd scraped together enough to buy his first car, she had spent the entire first ride bouncing on the seats and tuning in her favorite teenybopper songs on the radio. By the time he graduated from high school and left for college, she'd become a geeky high school sophomore obsessed with her grades and her crush on the cute quarterback.

It wasn't until three years later, when she arrived at his front door after her high school graduation, that he noticed how beautiful she'd become. Her coltish body had filled out and her gangly legs were now long and slender. When Maggie walked down the street at his side, that very first year in Chicago, people had turned to stare.

And they hadn't stopped looking since. He'd watched her grow into a smart and determined and beautiful woman. She'd graduated from the University of Chicago with a degree in botany, then immediately wrangled herself a government grant and a small business loan to start her floral shop on Clark Street in Lincoln Park. Through it all, she'd never lost that sweet vulnerability that had first drawn him to her.

Maybe that's what had affected him so strongly, standing on her porch and staring down into her eyes. He couldn't bear to see the pain in her expression, the humiliation in her eyes. So he'd returned her kiss, hoping that somehow he might make her feel better. Instead, he'd embarrassed them both by lapsing into lust.

Luke leaned back in his chair and raked his hands through his hair. It may have been an embarrassing moment, but he couldn't deny that he'd enjoyed kissing her. She'd felt so good in his arms, not at all like he expected. Whenever he thought of Maggie, the thoughts had always been tempered with images of her as a child. Now, he could barely remember the child she had been. Instead, his mind was filled with the taste and feel of the woman she was—a woman he wasn't supposed to want!

He groaned, then rubbed his eyes again. It was

nearly 4:00 a.m. His plane was due to leave in three hours. Usually, he was excited to start an assignment, especially with such potential as this one. But for some reason, Luke didn't feel like getting on a plane and leaving Chicago behind him. He had suddenly grown weary of living out of a suitcase, arguing with translators and swearing at satellite phones. And he'd grown tired of the whine of bullets and the menace of land mines.

Luke squinted at his computer screen and reached for the keyboard. "Get a grip, Fitzpatrick. Now is no time to go soft. You made an error in judgment. When you get back, you can smooth everything over with Maggie."

"Hey, what are you doing here? The party break up early?"

Luke spun his chair around and watched as his boss approached. Tom Wilcox had covered every war since Korea. He'd won the Pulitzer twice, once with the *L.A. Times* and once with the *Washington Post*. Now, at age seventy, he was in charge of a stable of hotshot writers and fearless photographers who only hoped to be as good as Wilcox was on his worst day.

"I left early and I didn't want to go home to sleep. Besides, I adjust to the time change better if I stay up all night. What about you? Don't tell me you're spending the turn of the millennium at work."

Tom chuckled. "I remember sitting in a hootch during the Tet Offensive, wondering if I'd ever see the next century. I made a promise to that old managing editor in the sky that if he got me through my tour in Nam, he could reassign me any time after midnight on December 31 in the year 1999."

"Knowing you, you'll be around for the next millennium celebration."

A serious expression clouded his boss's face. "You just listen up, Fitzpatrick. I want you to watch your six out there. Don't get into any situation where you need to start making promises like I did. No story is worth a dead reporter."

"Who else are you going to get to take these cushy assignments? I could be covering some diplomatic beat, sleeping in fancy hotels, eating hot food every day, taking an occasional shower. Instead, I get the pleasure of leaky tents, canned cuisine and smelly clothes."

"And you'd rather be there than anyplace else in the world."

Luke paused for a long moment. In truth, no, he didn't want to go to Albania. The biggest scoop of his journalistic career had been dropped in his lap, an exclusive interview with the leader of the rebel faction, and he was ready to throw it aside. Any one of his peers would kill for an opportunity like this. But right now, Luke wanted to stay in Chicago, close to Maggie.

His next thought was completely unplanned and completely out of character, but Luke voiced it anyway. "Actually, I'd like to talk to you about that, Tom. I was wondering whether I might delay my trip to Albania. Just for a few days. I'm not scheduled to meet Janaz until a week from Monday. And I've got some personal matters I need to take care of here."

Wilcox frowned, then laughed out loud. "Yeah, right. Come on, Fitzpatrick, don't joke around. You think those rebels operate on a timetable? I want you there, on the ground, ready to move."

"You could assign someone else," Luke suggested. "Just in case. Besides, they're not going to take me into the camp early."

"This is your interview. He agreed to see you."

"And he will. A week from Monday, like we planned."

Wilcox shook his head. "I'm sorry, Luke. This is the biggest story on the boards now. I can't risk losing it."

Luke cursed softly. He should let it go, but just couldn't. The more he thought about it, the more he knew he should stay in Chicago. Maggie had been through a terrible upheaval and he was the only one she could turn to now that Isabelle had betrayed her. And if he stayed, he might get to kiss her again.

Luke drew a sharp breath and wrote the last thought off to sheer exhaustion. "I can't go," he said, pushing to his feet. "Not now. I don't care what you say. Fire me if you have to, but I'm staying right here." He grabbed his jacket from the back of the chair, gathered up his papers and shoved them into the case with his laptop. "I'll call you day after tomorrow and we can work out my schedule then."

"Luke, don't force my hand," Wilcox warned. "We need this story."

He waved over his shoulder. "And I need some sleep. I'll talk to you later."

By the time he reached his truck, the sun was already turning the sky over Lake Michigan a deep blue. Some millennium parties were still in full swing and people stumbled along the sidewalks, dressed in fancy evening clothes that looked a bit disheveled compared to six hours before.

Luke headed north along the lakefront, crawling along with the traffic and listening to the news. After all the hype and dire predictions, Luke couldn't help but be disappointed at the actual event, the turning of the millennium. He'd spent the night at a stuffy party, had a few glasses of expensive champagne and chomped down a plateful of hors d'oeuvres.

A smile twitched at his mouth. But then he'd come to the aid of a beautiful woman. And there had been that kiss. Luke suspected that of all the memories from the millennium, he wouldn't forget the taste of Maggie's lips any time soon.

4

THE MILLENNIUM celebration hadn't ended by eight the next morning, nor had the problems with the power system. As Maggie drove her beat-up minivan to her flower shop on Clark Street, stray party-goers still stumbled along the sidewalks, bleary-eyed and searching for cars they might never find and crossing the street against stoplights that worked only occasionally. Every other business along her block was closed for New Year's Day, in recognition of the holiday and the lack of dependable electrical power, but Maggie had decided to go into the shop for a few hours.

She couldn't stay cooped up at home for another minute longer. Sleep had evaded her the previous night and she'd spent the time before dawn pacing the confines of the coach house until she'd covered every square inch of floor space. Her thoughts should have been occupied with Colin, with the shortest engagement in the history of romance. Instead, she'd spent her time trying to figure out a way to salvage her friendship with Luke Fitzpatrick.

Had he been any other man, she could put him out of her life without a second thought. But Luke was her only connection to her childhood and Maggie couldn't risk losing that. Her life had been built on such a fragile foundation, like a house of cards. To remove Luke would cause her past to disappear and the house to crumble.

Nothing—not even the prospect of passion and romance—could get her to risk that. Besides, Maggie knew that to fall in love with Luke would be foolish. Any romantic relationship they might have would only be fleeting and, ultimately, hopeless. Even Isabelle, who lost her heart as quickly as she changed her hairstyle, knew to save herself from loving Luke. He could never give Maggie the kind of life she wanted. In truth, he could barely manage to maintain their friendship.

They used to take long walks together and linger over coffee and doughnuts. In the winter, they'd skate at one of the city rinks—all habits that had begun when they were kids. They'd talk about anything and everything that made a difference in their lives. But in the past year, Maggie could count on one hand the hours they spent together. So she'd begun to rely on Luke less and less, aware that there would come a time when he'd fade from her life and become a part of her past. Maybe that's why she'd been so determined to marry Colin, to build a new life for herself.

Maggie pulled up to an unlit stoplight then proceeded through the intersection cautiously. Today, she'd catch up on her paperwork, prepare this week's order to her wholesaler and work on a design for the Valentine's window display. And when she was finished with that, she would find more work to do, anything to keep her mind off what had happened last night. Work had always been a refuge for her, blotting out any worries in her personal life.

As she turned the corner onto Clark, the real depth of her problems hit her square in the face. Her little store would be hers for only two months longer. After that, the quaint brick storefront would become a coffee shop, as if this neighborhood needed another outlet for caffeine and conversation.

No matter how she looked at it, she'd made a stupid business decision. At Colin's urging, Maggie had decided to take a risk with her business, agreeing to move her shop from Clark Street to the lobby of the Spencer Center. But the risks had been outweighed by so many benefits. Her corporate clients were all downtown, the Spencer Center space on Michigan Avenue had five times more foot traffic than her Clark Street location and Colin had given her a substantial break on the rent. With this in mind, taking out a bank loan to set up the new shop hadn't seemed like such a rash decision.

Everything had been arranged before the engagement—or rather, the broken engagement. Now there was no question in her mind that all agreements and arrangements were moot. How could she possibly work in the same building as Colin, running the risk of seeing him every day? And how could he justify keeping on a tenant, an ex-fiancée that paid only half what the retail space was worth?

"I need a plan," she murmured as she pulled up in front of the building. "I should talk to Luke. He'd know what to do."

But she couldn't ask Luke! Not anymore. After last night, he'd become part of the problem. She was a grown woman and it was time to stop depending on Luke to rescue her from every major dilemma in her life.

When Colin had proposed, Maggie had brushed aside the instinct to discuss it with Luke. Instead, she had accepted Colin's proposal, certain that she'd weighed the pros and cons carefully. Maggie turned off the engine and yanked the keys from the ignition. Maybe her decision-making skills weren't all they should be, but she'd tried. This time she was determined to do a better job of planning her future.

She slammed the van door then bundled herself against the cold wind as she ran to the front door of the shop. When she looked up, Maggie stopped dead in her tracks. A man stood in the shadows of the shop doorway. Her heart skipped and she swallowed hard. She wasn't ready to speak to Colin, not now, not yet.

But the figure that stepped out of the doorway wasn't Colin, it was Luke—the only person in the world she wanted to see *less* than Colin. Memories of last night's kiss rushed through her. Maggie pasted a smile on her face and feigned a nonchalant attitude, but her heart hammered in her chest and her knees felt weak. Maybe if she acted as if the kiss had never happened, they could just forget it. "Luke! What are you doing here?"

"I thought we could take a walk," he said, stepping toward her and reaching for her hand. "We need to talk."

For a moment, she couldn't breathe. Though she'd looked at Luke millions of times in the past, she felt as if she were staring at him through a stranger's eyes. He wore jeans, a chambray shirt and faded field coat. She'd always chided him for his wardrobe, but suddenly, what once looked careless, now seemed incredibly sexy and comfortingly familiar.

His hair, which she usually considered a bit too long, now brushed his collar at the perfect length, dark and thick and blown by the brisk winter wind. And Maggie had never noticed what an unusual shade his eyes were, an odd mixture of blue and gray. Even though he looked as though he hadn't slept at all, Maggie thought he was probably the most handsome man she'd ever known.

She swallowed hard and avoided Luke's touch. There was a time when she had thought Colin was the most handsome man in the world. When had that changed? When she'd seen him walk out of the Spencer Center with Isabelle on his arm? Or had it been later, when Luke had yanked her into his arms and kissed her?

"I thought you were off to Albania," Maggie said, reaching around him to unlock the front door of the shop. "Did they cancel the revolution?"

His expression was grim. "I couldn't leave. Not with everything that's happened."

She reached for the security system and turned off the alarm, thankful that her block of Clark Street still had electricity. "And what has happened?" she asked, stalking through the store to the rear workroom.

Luke reached out and grabbed her elbow, catching her this time. She wanted to pull away, but she liked the feel of his hands on her, the warmth of his fingers seeping through her coat. "Maggie, I know you must be upset. And I certainly didn't help things with my behavior last night. I just wanted to be here in case you needed me."

"Needed you?"

"To talk," he said.

She tugged off her coat and tossed it over the counter. "What happened between us was a...a lapse in judgment. I was emotionally overwrought. And what happened with Colin is my problem, not yours. So you can go to Albania. You don't have to worry about me. I can take care of myself."

"Your problems are my problems."

Maggie felt her frustration rise. She turned, and leaned back against the counter. "Ever since we were kids, you've looked out for me. And for every major decision in my life, I came to you for advice—what college to attend, what major to choose, where to open my flower shop. And I'm grateful for your help. But I'm the one who agreed to marry Colin. And I'm the one who will have to decide if I can forgive him or not."

Luke braced his hands on either side of her, trapping her against the counter, his gaze fierce. "Forgive him? Geez, Maggie, he ran off with your best friend! You can't actually be thinking about forgiving him, can you?"

Of course she didn't plan to forgive Colin. But Luke didn't need to know that. "I—I'm not sure what really happened," Maggie replied, uneasy with his nearness, yet wanting him to come even closer. "And until I have a chance to talk to him, we're still engaged. So—so you can go to Albania. I'll be all right."

"Maggie, why are you doing this? Colin obviously is not the man for you. You shouldn't even consider taking him back."

"Where did you get the idea that you can run my life?" she asked, pushing at his arm and breaking free. "I've seen you—what?—maybe four times in the past year? I hear more about your life from Isabelle than I do from you."

A current of jealousy shot through her and her anger at Isabelle doubled. She'd stolen her best friend *and* her fiancé! And Maggie had allowed it. But it wasn't just Isabelle that she was angry at. It was Luke. He was the one who had let their friendship flounder. He was the one off traveling the world leaving her to fend for herself. And he was the one whose kisses had turned her world completely upside down!

"Is that what this is about? Did you agree to marry Spencer because I wasn't paying enough attention to you?"

Maggie forced a sharp laugh. "You do have an ego, don't you?" But as ridiculous as his words first struck her, she couldn't help wondering if there was a shard of truth in his accusation. If Luke had been around, would she have accepted Colin's proposal? Would she have settled for a loveless marriage so quickly? "The entire world doesn't revolve around you," she continued. "As for my life, that stopped revolving around you long ago."

"Maggie, if you want to get angry at me, then—"

"Here's a news flash, Luke Fitzpatrick. This is none of your business. Now, I think you should go. I have a lot of work to do."

"I'm not leaving," Luke said, his jaw set stubbornly. "Not until we talk about what happened between us."

Maggie sighed and shook her head, suddenly desperate to send him on his way. She couldn't defend herself, not under his ceaseless onslaught. She'd never been able to lie to Luke, and she was dancing perilously close to deception now. She *did* want him in her life and his kiss *did* mean something! "It was nothing," she lied.

"Are you sure?"

With a soft curse, she grabbed his face between her palms and kissed him square on the mouth. Just as quickly, she pulled back and sent him a smug smile. "See? We've kissed each other hundreds of times before just like that and nothing has happened. Nothing."

He stared at her, his gaze fixed on hers. A flicker of desire darkened his eyes and a slow shiver worked its way down her spine. It took less than a second to realize her mistake. How could she have done something so reckless, provoking him like this?

He bent closer and her breath caught in her throat.

Maggie knew she should turn away. But she needed to appease her curiosity and prove to herself that last night *was* just a minor lapse. "Go ahead," Maggie challenged. "I won't feel anything. What happened last night didn't mean a thing."

With a soft curse, he lowered his mouth to hers in a languid kiss. Slowly, deliberately, he explored her mouth and teased at her lips with his tongue. Maggie had every opportunity to pull away, but she couldn't. Desire rushed through her like a current, pulsing in her veins until every nerve in her body vibrated with need.

She'd never been kissed like this in her life, never given herself over to the feeling of a man's mouth on hers. Every sensation was intensely new yet so perfect. She didn't feel clumsy or uneasy, she felt as if she could throw open her arms and float up to the clouds.

And even if she wanted to stop, she couldn't. She'd lost all capacity to reason, lost all touch with reality. Her reality had become this kiss and only this kiss, the warmth of Luke's lips, the strength of his hands kneading her arms, the scent of his cologne, the sound of his breathing, quick and heavy.

When Luke finally drew away, Maggie opened her eyes and her world came crashing down around her. With a soft cry, she brought her fingers to her lips as if she'd been burned.

"Tell me that didn't mean anything, Maggie."

She swallowed hard, unable to speak at first. "It—it didn't mean anything," she stammered.

His eyes narrowed and his jaw went tight, her words a blatant betrayal of the trust they'd always shared. "Yeah, you're right. It didn't mean anything. It was like kissing my...grandmother."

His words pierced her heart and she bit her lip to keep it from trembling. How had their friendship shattered so quickly and so completely? Maggie used to be able to say anything to Luke, but since that awful moment last night, their relationship seemed to be teetering on the edge of destruction.

"I just want things to be the way they used to," Maggie said, emotion clogging her throat until she could barely speak.

"They'll never be the same, Maggie. We can't go back."

"Why not? We can just forget all this and be friends again. And when Colin comes back..."

"You're going to go back to him."

Maggie shook her head. "I don't know that. I at least owe him a chance to explain."

"And will you explain what happened between us?"

Maggie sighed. "Whatever I decide to do, it will be my decision." She looked up at him. "Go to Albania or wherever it is you're supposed to be. And when you come back, everything will be all right. I promise."

He raked his fingers through his hair. "Promise me you won't go back to him. That you won't agree to marry him before we have another chance to talk."

"I already agreed to marry him," Maggie said softly, holding out her hand to show him the ring.

With a soft curse, he turned and strode to the door. He paused once on his way out, then shook his head and yanked open the door. When he was finally gone, Maggie breathed a long sigh of relief and slowly sank to the floor. She leaned back against the counter and closed her eyes.

Confusion gripped her mind and she tried to sort out the chaos, examining her feelings objectively. Could Luke be right? Had she agreed to marry Colin, in part, because she wanted to get Luke's attention? Did she want him to ride in and save her from a loveless marriage, to play the hero once more?

Maggie had never really examined her feelings for Luke. She'd always assumed that there was nothing more between them than familial affection. If there was more, why had she introduced Isabelle to Luke? Maggie opened her eyes as an unwelcome realization struck her.

Maybe she knew all along that Isabelle was a safe choice for Luke. Who better than a woman who was incapable of sustaining a permanent relationship? She buried her face in her hands. Everything had been so simple just a few days ago. Luke and Isabelle had been her friends and Colin had been the man she was going to marry.

Now, all of that had changed. And Maggie suspected that no matter what she did, no matter how much she wished it, she couldn't put things back the way they had been.

THE FREEWAY out to O'Hare was clogged with traffic and the taxi had come to a dead stop behind an endless line of cars and trucks. Luke checked his watch every few minutes, anxious about making his flight. He could have waited until later that night for a more direct flight into Athens. But the sooner he got out of Chicago, the better. Being in the same city as Maggie had suddenly become more of a complication than a convenience.

The only way to put her out of his mind was to put seven thousand miles between them. Maybe then, he'd be able to get back to focusing on his work. Luke leaned back in the seat and closed his eyes. Instead of stark images of Eastern Europe, his mind flashed back to the kiss he'd shared with Maggie less than an hour ago.

Nothing. That's what she'd claimed to feel when she kissed him. No more than sisterly affection. Luke had never been very adept at reading a woman's thoughts, but with Maggie he'd always known what was in her mind—except this time. He had a hard time believing that a connection so charged with attraction had caused no reaction at all. That certainly hadn't been the case on *his* end of the kiss. Any thought of Maggie Kelley in a sisterly light had disappeared last night on her front porch. Hell, he'd enjoyed kissing her. He wanted to do it again—and soon!

And that's why he'd decided to get out of town. His boss had been thrilled that Luke had decided to go after all, and a few quick calls had been all it took to change his plane ticket. Maggie wasn't the only one desperate to set things back on a normal track.

He took a sip from the Starbucks cup he clutched, the strong coffee burning his mouth. He'd always understood Maggie so well. But in the same instant he started looking at her as something more than a sister, she'd suddenly become a stranger to him. Why had she decided to marry Colin without even mentioning it to him? They barely knew each—Luke stopped and shook his head.

It seemed like just yesterday when he'd stopped into Maggie's shop with his old buddy, Colin. His motives had been purely selfish—Maggie hadn't had a date in nearly a year and he was beginning to feel a little guilty about constantly canceling their plans. He thought an introduction to Colin Spencer might soothe his guilt.

Just yesterday, Luke mused. But it hadn't been yesterday. Maggie had been with Colin for almost two years, years that Luke had spent covering wars and uprisings and skirmishes. Two years had slipped by without him noticing, without realizing that he was losing a piece of himself—he was losing Maggie.

The cab pulled up in front of the international terminal at O'Hare and jerked to a stop. Luke paid the cabbie, hopped out and grabbed his garment bag and computer case from the trunk. He'd learned to travel light—a couple of changes of clothing, his shaving kit, an extra pair of comfortable shoes and his laptop with its satellite hookup. He could write a story in Albania and have it on the wire within minutes of finishing it.

He walked through the sliding glass doors and into the terminal. As he hoisted his bag up on his shoulder, his cell phone rang. He pulled the phone out of his jacket pocket and plugged his ear against the chatter of voices around him.

"Fitzpatrick," he said, expecting to hear Tom Wilcox's voice on the other end, giving him last-minute instructions.

"Luke! It's me, Colin."

At first, he thought he'd misheard. The connection wasn't good, fading in and out. But then the voice on the other end of the line said his name again. "Spencer?" How the hell did Colin get his cell-phone number?

"Yeah, it's me. I called your office and told them it was a family emergency. They gave me this number. Where are you?"

"I'm at the airport. Where the hell are you?"

"That doesn't make a difference. I need you to do me a favor."

"I'll beat the crap out of you, how about that?" Luke shouted in the phone. "That would be a big favor for all of us. How could you do that to Maggie? How could you just walk out on her without any warning?"

"That's why I called. I need you to keep an eye out for her. I just need a little time to straighten out a few things and then I'm coming back. I'll explain everything then."

He dropped his bags at his feet. "What? You still plan to marry her?"

"Yeah," Colin said. "I do."

Luke's grip tightened on the phone. "Go to hell, Spencer." He flipped the phone off and shoved it back into his pocket, then snatched his bags off the floor. He took only a few more steps before he stopped. It was always so easy to leave on assignment in the past, but this time he found every step toward the ticket counter agonizing. This time he wanted to stay, but not only to look after Maggie. No, his reasons were much less honorable. He wanted to stay so he could figure out *why* he wanted to stay.

Try as he might, he couldn't keep his mind off her. But why now, after all this time? If he'd had serious feelings for her, why hadn't he realized earlier? Luke raked his fingers through his hair and turned to look back in the direction of the taxi stand. Maybe it was because Maggie had decided to get married. Maybe the thought of losing her to another man had been enough to force him to face up to his feelings.

So what were his feelings? Was he in love with Maggie Kelley? Or did he just want what he couldn't have? He knew whenever he was with Maggie, he had a better sense of himself. He grew up with her by his side. While most children had parents and siblings who knew them inside and out, Luke had Maggie. She was his touchstone, the connection to who he was and where he came from. Without her, he had no past.

But with her, he had no future. Maggie had always wanted a family of her own. She had talked about her dreams from the time he first knew her—a big house, a devoted husband and children, lots of children. She'd been desperate to find what she'd missed in her own childhood: stability and security.

And those were the only two things that Luke could never give her. He was never sure where he would be from day to day, his schedule dependent on whatever world crisis popped up. And the press syndicate didn't pay well enough to buy a house in Kenilworth or on the North Shore...a house that Maggie would have if she married Colin.

Maybe she was better off with Spencer. Plenty of guys screwed up and managed to find forgiveness and carry on. Who was he to interfere in Maggie's life? She had every right to make her own decisions, every right to forgive Colin for his sins.

Luke hoisted his bags up on his shoulder and took another few steps toward the check-in counter. But once again, his instincts told him to stop and go back. Go back to Maggie, to something much more important than a story about a revolution halfway around the world. Go back for a chance to find out what she really meant to him.

He stood near the doors for a long time, pulled one way by his professional standards and another way by his personal confusion.

In the end, he made the only decision he could, a decision he'd made again and again on battlefields and in war zones all over the world. Luke decided to go with his instincts.

MAGGIE TURNED OFF the lights in the shop and wearily opened the front door. Though the shop had been closed to customers, she was still exhausted. The power had flickered on and off all day long, sending her computer and her phone into fits of bizarre activity. Teleflora had sent her the same order over and over again until the fax machine had run out of paper. Her security alarm went off every time the power dropped. And her computer crashed whenever she tried to enter today's date, even though she'd paid a consultant a pretty penny to debug the system. All and all, the millennium had managed to mess up every facet of her miserable life.

As Maggie turned to walk to her van, a limousine pulled up in front of the shop. The tinted rear window whirred down and Eunice Spencer popped her head out and waved cheerfully. "Maggie, dear! I've been looking all over for you! Where have you been?"

Maggie frowned and glanced back at her shop. "I—I've been working," she said.

Eunice looked positively perplexed. "You work? Whatever for?" She waited for the chauffeur to open the door and help her out of the car. She wore another of her fur coats, a white mink, this one making her look like a short, stout polar bear with a fondness for expensive jewelry. "I don't think I like the notion of my future daughter-in-law toiling in some—some—" She flipped her hand in the direction of the shop. "Where is it you work?"

"I'm a floral designer," Maggie explained. "And this is my shop."

Eunice looked over the shop with a disdainful expression, then grabbed Maggie's hand. "Never mind about that. I came here because I have news. Come, I'll give you a ride home."

"But I have my van," Maggie said. "It's right here."

Colin's mother grabbed her hand and pulled her toward the limo. "Then take a little ride with me. I have something to show you."

Reluctantly, Maggie got into the limo. Once inside, Eunice handed her a flute of champagne and smiled. "We know where Colin is and we know how he got there."

Maggie really didn't want to discuss Colin, but trapped as she was, she wasn't sure she could refuse. Short of hopping out at the next stoplight, Maggie would be forced to hear everything Eunice had to say.

"He took the Spencer jet," Eunice said. "Hamilton, our family's chauffeur, drove him down to the airport."

"The Spencers have a jet?"

Eunice stared as if Maggie had suddenly grown horns on the top of her head. "Of course we do! We keep it down at Meigs Field. As I was saying, Colin took the jet. Now, we weren't sure where he went until the pilot got back this morning. It seems my son has taken a little jaunt to Las Vegas. We have private investigators flying out there as we speak to track him down. We're watching his credit-card receipts, his phone calls. I'm sure he'll be back home by the end of the day."

"Mrs. Spencer, I—"

"Call me Eunice, dear. There's no need for formality. We're almost family, you know."

"That's what I wanted to speak to you—"

Eunice held up her hand and shook her head. "I know you're concerned, but I want you to know that Mr. Spencer and I plan to make sure that Colin follows through on this engagement."

"Follows through?"

"Colin had too much to drink. He wasn't himself. And with all the pressures at work, it's no wonder he...he—"

"Cracked?" Maggie asked.

Eunice sniffed, then neatly folded her hands on her lap. "I suppose you could say that. Not that my son has any mental problems. There have never been mental problems in the Spencer family. This was just a little…"

"Lapse in judgment?" Maggie asked, recalling her own words.

"Yes," Eunice said, obviously pleased with the description. "A lapse in judgment. A lapse that can easily be forgiven if Colin makes the proper apologies. He made a promise to you and he's going to keep it. That's all there is to it."

"Mrs. Spen—" Maggie took a deep breath. "Eunice, you seem to have forgotten that Colin ran off with another woman."

"Oats," Eunice said. "That's all she is. Oats."

"Oats?"

"He's sowing his wild oats, dear. Believe me, before Edward married me he sowed enough oats to feed half the cattle in Kansas. It's just something that Spencer men do. But after the wedding, I put an end to the harvest and told him to keep his seed in the silo."

A tiny smile quirked the corners of Maggie's mouth. She'd always considered Eunice a first-class snob. Glancing out the window of the limo, she noticed they were headed downtown on LaSalle. A few moments later, the driver turned onto Oak. "Where are we going?" she asked.

"It's a surprise," Eunice said.

The car pulled up in front of a row of shops and Hamilton quickly opened the door and helped them both out. Eunice linked her arm through Maggie's, as if they'd suddenly become fast friends. The older woman led her along the sidewalk, carefully avoiding the icy patches, then stopped. "Here we are!"

Maggie looked up at the shop windows and her heart fell. "A bridal shop?"

"Not just any bridal shop," Eunice said. "This is Simone's. It's the *only* bridal shop in Chicago—the only shop that sells dresses suitable for a Spencer bride. Come, dear. I had them open especially for us. We're going to pick out your wedding gown! Won't this be fun?"

Maggie groaned inwardly. Her wedding gown? Eunice had to be joking! Less than twenty-four hours ago, Colin had run off with another woman. And not just any woman, but Maggie's best friend. Oats or no oats, his behavior would indicate a strong aversion to becoming a groom. As for the mental problems, Maggie was beginning to think that Eunice was the certifiable Spencer.

"Don't you think we ought to wait until Colin returns before we go ahead with wedding plans?"

"Spilt milk," Eunice said.

"What?"

"There's no use crying over spilt milk. As far as I'm concerned, we've mopped up the floor and moved on."

Maggie opened her mouth to protest, then snapped it shut. There had to be a way to get out of this gracefully. Telling Eunice that she had no intention of marrying Colin would only cause the woman to redouble her efforts. But if she went along with her, she'd be walking out of Simone's with a dress she'd never wear. "Could we do this some other time? I—I'm really tired. I didn't sleep much last night and I—"

Eunice clucked her tongue and dragged Maggie toward the door. "Oh, fiddle," she muttered.

"Fiddle-dee-dee?"

"No, dear. Why fiddle while Rome burns?" Eunice

asked. "Instead, we're going to plan your wedding." With that, she dragged Maggie into the shop.

Simone's was everything Eunice had promised. Three saleswomen attended them, waltzing back and forth with incredibly beautiful lace and silk gowns. Maggie patiently listened to descriptions of seed pearls and Belgian lace, ten-foot trains and sweetheart necklines. After nearly an hour of listening to Eunice's opinion on each design, Maggie decided to put an end to their little shopping excursion. She chose the next gown offered, then at Eunice's insistence, stepped into the fitting room to try it on.

The trio of saleswomen helped her undress, then carefully maneuvered her into the gown. The dress was a beautiful creation of silk shantung. The hand-beaded bodice fit her as if it were made for her, and the neckline, cut deep, framed her face. When the final button had been fastened along her spine, Maggie stepped back and stared into the mirror.

The reflection that stared back at her took her breath away. She'd never seen anything so incredible, so absolutely perfect. She looked like a fairy-tale princess, an image that came straight from her childhood dreams. "It's beautiful," she said, her words slipping out on a sigh.

"Is this the one, then?" one of the saleswomen asked.

Maggie nodded, pressing her fingertips to her lips. "Can I be alone for a moment?"

The saleswoman nodded to her two associates and they slipped out of the fitting room, but Maggie barely noticed them leave. Her attention was completely captured by the reflection in the mirror. Tipping her head back, she closed her eyes.

An image of a wedding swam through her mind, the

candlelit church, the extravagant flowers, the music echoing through air…and the groom, waiting for her at the altar. The vision came into sudden focus and she saw Luke standing—

Maggie's eyes snapped open and her breath caught in her throat. "No!" she cried. With a frantic moan, she twisted her arm around her waist and tried to unbutton the back of the dress. But the buttons were too tiny and too numerous to handle. Frustrated, she sank onto the floor and buried her face in her hands.

What was going on in her head? "I'm just a little tired," Maggie told herself. "And this whole thing has gotten way out of hand." She hadn't meant to insert Luke into her fantasy. She hadn't intended to have a fantasy at all! Especially after everything that had happened.

A few kisses from Luke and she was ready to turn him into her dream husband—despite the fact that he didn't trust her to make her own decisions, that after disappearing from her life for months at a time, he insisted on telling her who she could and couldn't marry. The last thing he wanted was a lovesick bride to tie him down.

So he had managed to set her senses spinning with just a few simple kisses. That didn't mean she had to marry him! Maggie glanced up into the mirror and examined her reflection. She wasn't unattractive, but she certainly wasn't the kind of woman Luke usually gravitated toward. He liked gorgeous, sexy women with perfect figures and alluring attitudes. He saw her as his little sister, at the opposite end of the spectrum from sexy.

"Is everything all right?"

She turned to see one of the saleswomen standing in the doorway, watching her quizzically. Maggie scrambled to her feet and backed toward her. "Get me out of this dress," she demanded. "Now!"

The moment the last button was unfastened, Maggie tugged the gown from her shoulders, pushed it past her waist and stepped out of it. Then she snatched up her clothes and quickly dressed. By the time she escaped the fitting room, the gown had been returned to its hanger. Eunice stood in the middle of the shop, examining the detailed bodice with a finicky eye.

The instant she saw Maggie, she frowned. "Maggie, dear, are you sure this is the gown you want? Now that I've had a chance to look at it, I just don't think it's…elegant enough." She glanced down at the price tag and sniffed. "In for a penny," she said, shaking her head.

"In for a pound?" Maggie asked.

"Exactly my point. I mean, a Spencer bride should walk down the aisle in a dress designed especially for her, not a dress some other girl might be wearing. And we can certainly afford more than nine thousand for a dress."

Maggie's eyes went wide. "Nine thousand dollars? That dress costs nine thousand dollars? That's more than I paid for my van."

"You're absolutely right," Eunice said. "We can do better. In fact, why don't we fly to New York tomorrow morning and visit a few designers. And if we don't find a proper gown there, we'll go to Paris."

"I—I have to go," Maggie said, stalking through the shop to the door. "I'll call you. Soon."

"But dear," Eunice said, "I have an appointment with a wedding consultant. We have to discuss guest lists and reception plans. And what about china patterns?"

"We'll do that another time." Maggie grabbed the

door and quickly slipped outside. She paused only to draw a quick breath before hurrying to the corner. To her relief, she caught the first cab that passed.

Maggie crawled into the back and sunk down in the seat. "I have to get out of here," she murmured. "I can't stay here."

She'd never really considered how wealthy the Spencer family was. Sure, they owned a huge office tower on Michigan Avenue and a lot of other real estate around the city. But she'd almost married into a family that owned its own jet...and threw lavish parties for hundreds of snooty people...and spent five figures on a wedding gown!

"What was I thinking?" Maggie muttered.

"I don't know, lady, but I ain't got telepathic powers. Tell me where you're goin' or get outta my cab."

"Clark Street," she said to the cabbie. "Two blocks south of Diversey."

As the cab sped off, Maggie considered her options. If she stayed in Chicago, Eunice would continue to dog her every step, lobbying for a wedding that was never going to—

Maggie's heart skipped and she sat up. "It's never going to happen," she said out loud, as if hearing the words made them true. "I'm not going to marry Colin Spencer." Nothing he could possibly say to her would make a difference. Because when all was said and done, Maggie couldn't possibly marry a man she didn't love.

She smiled to herself, pleased with her decision. Now all she had to do was make sure she didn't fall in love with a man she could never marry.

5

MAGGIE LEANED OVER and tugged on her skates, then quickly threaded the laces through the eyes and hooks. Her warm breath clouded in front of her face and the brisk evening air chilled her cheeks. The skating rink on State Street was one of her favorite winter spots in the city. Set in the midst of busy downtown, the rink served as a festive break from the leaden skies and concrete skyscrapers that dominated the Loop. Elaborate department-store lights and decorations from Marshall Field could be seen from the ice, and cheery music echoed from speakers above the rink.

She and Luke had first skated here years ago on New Year's Day. Every winter she looked forward to their "date," to a time when she had Luke all to herself and she could start the new year with a smile. They had made plans to skate again this very evening, but Luke had canceled a few days ago because of his assignment in Albania. Maggie had been disappointed at the time, but after all that had happened, she wasn't really anxious to spend any more time with Luke.

She pushed up from the bench and skimmed out toward the center of the ice, slowly regaining her comfort on the smooth surface. As she stroked around in a lazy circle, Maggie couldn't help remembering the first time she'd put on skates. Luke had found an old pair at a secondhand shop and bought them for her for Christmas. He'd been thirteen and she'd been ten and he'd spent the astounding amount of three dollars on her gift, money he'd scrimped from his paper route. The skates had been her very favorite gift that year, even though the blades were nicked and the leather boots were cracked.

A tiny smile curled her lips as the memories came flooding back. They had skated at Fireman's Park in Potter's Junction, on a patch of ice the town cleared every winter on the shore of the lake. The lake wasn't nearly as nice as the glassy, groomed surface of the State Street rink, but it was a perfect place to pass an evening, away from the chaos of her mother's house. She could still smell the tang of the wood-burning stove in the rink's warming house, still feel the burn of hot chocolate on her tongue and the bite of the wind on her skin.

She and Luke would skate until they were nearly frozen to the bone, then they'd huddle in the warming house and sip hot cocoa from a thermos she'd brought from home. After the feeling returned to their fingers and toes, Luke would walk her home and leave her at the front door, exhausted and happy.

Life had been so simple back then. She hadn't been plagued with doubts and regrets. Luke was her friend and that was all there was to it. Nothing he did could alter her undying affection for him.

"If only I could go back to that time," Maggie murmured, slowing her speed to avoid an older couple skating in front of her. Just a few days ago, Luke had still been her friend, but now she wasn't even sure she liked him. How was a girl supposed to feel when he all but admitted he didn't find her sexually attractive? When kissing her was no more exciting than planting a kiss on his grandmother's cheek?

With a frustrated moan, Maggie picked up her pace

and began to speed around the rink, easily weaving in and out among the other skaters. But she didn't anticipate the small group of boys with hockey sticks cutting across the center of the rink. She cried out a warning, but there was no time to stop or steer clear. One of the sticks caught her skate blade and before she knew it, she was skidding across the ice on her stomach. She came to a stop against a low wall and then, groaning, she rolled over and sat up.

The crisp sound of skate blades came up behind her and she waited for one of the rink attendants to help her up. A hand appeared over her shoulder and she took it, but when she got to her feet it wasn't an attendant she had to thank.

"You still haven't learned to stop, have you?" Luke grinned down at her, his cheeks ruddy with the cold, his thick hair blown back off his face by the wind.

Maggie's heart tripped at the sight of him, but she chose to ignore the feeling. "What are you doing here?"

"I stopped by your house to see you and then went over to the shop. You weren't there either, so I made an educated guess. Don't you remember? It's New Year's Day. We always skate on New Year's Day."

"You canceled," Maggie said, dusting off her backside. "Don't *you* remember?"

"And now I'm here. Let's skate."

Maggie shook her head, moving back into the crowd that circled the rink. But Luke was at her side in a matter of minutes. He jumped in front of her, then turned easily on his hockey skates and sent her a devilish smile, easily stroking backward as he spoke.

She ignored a shiver that skittered down her spine, writing it off to her damp rear end. He wore a faded hockey jersey with a Chicago Blackhawks emblem on the front and a pair of threadbare jeans with a hole in the knee. His face was covered with a dark stubble of beard and his pale blue eyes glinted beneath the bright lights surrounding the rink. Compared to Colin's fastidious appearance, Luke looked completely disreputable—and undeniably sexy.

"I pushed back my trip to Albania," he explained. "Twice, actually."

"Why would you do that?"

"So I could come skating with you," he said. He caught her hands in his and drew her over the ice. His fingers were warm around hers, even though he didn't wear gloves. For a moment, she considered pulling away from him. The flood of attraction that raced through her was more than she could handle. But in the end, Maggie skated silently, stealing looks at him whenever he glanced over his shoulder to steer them around other skaters.

"I'm glad I found you," he said, leading them to the edge of the ice. "There's something I had to tell you."

Maggie shook her head. "I really don't want to hear anything else from you."

He pulled her toward the edge of the ice, tugged her down on a bench and turned to her. When she refused to look at him, Luke grabbed her chin between his fingers and forced her gaze up to his face. "I wasn't being honest with you. Not last night on the porch and not earlier today at your shop."

"I'm not sure I want to hear the truth," Maggie said, staring down at a hole in the thumb of her mitten. "The lies were embarrassing enough."

He pressed her hands between his. "Well, here it is. I did feel something when I kissed you."

"You—you did?"

He nodded, then drew a deep breath. "I guess, I

didn't want to admit it, but I...I enjoyed kissing you, Maggie."

A tiny thrill raced through her. "Why *did* you kiss me?"

"Because you kissed me first," Luke said.

"That's not an answer."

He tipped his head back and smiled. "The hell if I know. Curiosity, maybe. Or maybe I thought it would make you feel better. But you have to understand I would never do anything to harm our friendship. You're the closest thing I have to family and I don't want to jeopardize that. And if you're still set on marrying Colin, I want you to know I'll stand behind you. And if you want, we can go look for Colin. I've got a week before I have to leave again."

"Eunice came to the shop earlier. She said he went to Las Vegas. Why would he go to Vegas?"

Luke shrugged. "He's with Isabelle. Who knows what influence she's exerted on him."

"Do you really think he didn't want to marry me?"

Luke paused for a long moment and stared out across the ice. "I don't know what Spencer is thinking."

"I know what his mother has on her mind," Maggie said with a rueful grin. "She took me shopping for a wedding gown this afternoon. And before long, she'll have me looking at china, crystal and silver patterns. Eunice is certain this wedding will still happen."

"And what do you want?" Luke asked quietly.

Maggie pressed her palms into her knees and shrugged. She could tell him the truth, that she had no intention of marrying Colin. That she wanted him instead. But that was a fantasy, an impossibility. "Right now, I don't know what I want." She looked over at Luke. "Maybe I didn't love him enough."

He frowned at her sudden confession. "Colin?"

"Or maybe he never loved me."

"Then why would he ask you to marry him?"

"Love isn't the only reason to get married," she said, looking away from Luke and gazing at a pair of skaters circling the rink. "We could have had a good marriage. Solid. Dependable. But now I'm not so sure. How dependable is a guy who runs off to Vegas with his fiancée's best friend? What I don't understand is, why Isabelle? I didn't think Colin even liked her."

"I wish I knew."

"I'm not blaming her," Maggie said. "Not entirely. In fact, I've decided not to place any blame until I know exactly what happened. I keep going over it in my mind, trying to figure out what went wrong, but everything just gets more confusing the more I think about it."

They sat together, silently, for a long time, both of them watching the skaters glide around the rink. He took her hand and for the first time since Colin had walked out on her, she felt content. Sitting here with Luke, she could push away the present and retreat into the past, to a time when her life wasn't so complicated, to that little patch of ice on the lake in Potter's Junction.

"Are we still friends?" she asked.

Luke gave her a sideways glance and grinned. Then he held out his little finger.

Maggie pulled off her mitten, then hooked hers in his. "Pinkie promise," she said. "No more kissing. It really messes things up."

Luke gazed into her eyes for a long moment and she thought he might refuse the request. In truth, she hoped he would refuse and kiss her right here and now.

"All right," he agreed. "No more kissing."

"And one more thing," Maggie said. "Now that we're friends again, I think you should go to Albania."

"Maggie, I—"

She reached up and pressed her fingers to his lips. "Luke, I appreciate your concern, but you have a career to think about. This assignment sounds important."

"Not more important than you," he said.

"That's very sweet, but I'm a big girl. I can deal with my own problems."

He stood up and grabbed her hands, then yanked her to her feet. "Come on, let's make a few more laps around the rink."

They skated for another two hours and Maggie tried her best to ignore the feel of his hands on her waist, his fingers tangled with hers, the rough scrape of his beard on her cheek. He touched her without thinking, the way he always had. But it was different now. Every time they came in contact, her blood warmed and all her resolve wavered.

How could they possibly go back to being friends if his mere touch made her reel with desire? As the night went on, the cold seeped into her bones, creating a pleasant numbness and a welcome exhaustion. If she could just hang on for a little while longer, Luke would be on a plane to the other side of the world and she'd have a chance to put this ridiculous infatuation behind her.

Finally, she decided to call it a night. Luke walked her to the El and they said goodbye on the platform. To Maggie's relief, he didn't try to kiss her. If he had, she might have thrown her arms around his neck and relived her memories from the night before. Instead, she stepped onto the train and waited while the doors closed between them.

By the time Maggie got back to the coach house and crawled into bed, she'd nearly convinced herself that she and Luke could salvage their friendship. But as she stared at the ceiling above her bed, Maggie was bothered by one nagging realization, one thought she couldn't put out of her head. Now that they were friends again, how was she ever going to stop loving him?

THE SUN WAS UP when Maggie opened her eyes. She squinted at the bedside clock, then flopped over on her stomach and moaned softly. It was only 8:00 a.m.! She'd fallen asleep just two hours before, after tossing and turning the night away.

Closing her eyes, she tried to drift back to sleep. But thoughts of the day ahead intruded on her rest and, after a few minutes, she sat up in bed. Today was the day to put her plan into action. First, she'd push every thought of Luke right out of her head. Then, she'd call Eunice and tell her she had no intention of marrying her son, no matter what excuses he might come up with.

Colin had been AWOL for over twenty-four hours. He hadn't called, he hadn't sent a message. Except for the news Eunice provided, Maggie wouldn't even know if he were dead or alive. What had ever possessed her to consider marriage to a man she didn't love? Maggie pressed her fists to her eyes. "Was there a faster way to make a complete mess of my personal life?" she muttered.

She rolled out of bed and tugged on her chenille bathrobe. As she walked into the kitchen, she squinted through the window at the thermometer. "Fifteen degrees," she said. "Thank goodness I've got power."

She flipped on the television and listened to the

morning news as she made a pot of coffee. The millennium bug had bitten Chicago, though not as hard as predicted. The sporadic power outages that had plagued the city on New Year's Eve had now become just a nuisance. The phones were working and postal service promised that mail would be delivered on Monday. It seemed as if both the world and Maggie Kelley had survived the turning of the millennium.

Tugging her robe tighter, she grabbed a mug of steaming coffee and headed back to bed. As she was about to crawl beneath the covers, the doorbell rang. Maggie jumped at the sound, then took a moment to rake her fingers through her hair. Whoever it was at her door, she didn't want to see anyone. She hoped it was Luke, prayed it wasn't Eunice and knew it couldn't be Colin.

When she swung the door open, an icy blast hit her face. The Spencer family's chauffeur stood on the porch, his arms filled with boxes. Colin's mother peeked out from behind Hamilton and gave Maggie a cheery wave.

"Good morning, dear." She pushed past the driver and bustled inside, then impatiently motioned for him to follow. "We've got a lot of work to do. Hamilton, put those packages on the dining-room table. Miss Kelley and I have got an appointment in a few hours with the wedding consultant and then we're going to look at a few houses in Kenilworth."

Maggie gasped. "Houses?"

"Yes, dear. Edward and I are buying you a house for a wedding present. We can talk decorators at dinner."

She shook her head. This had to stop! "A house for a wedding present? What is this, a bribe?"

Eunice scowled. "Now that's a rather vulgar way to put it, but let's be honest, dear. Edward and I want our son to marry. He seems to have settled on you—that is, until that little piece of trash blew into his life."

"Her name is Isabelle," Maggie said, trying to school her temper. She'd never really liked Eunice, but she had tried to cultivate her good opinion. Now that the woman had turned into a first-class pest, Maggie couldn't care less what Eunice Spencer thought of her.

"At first, I wasn't happy about you," Eunice babbled, "but now I'm willing to forgo the lack of pedigree. After all, my father was the son of a butcher. But let me enlighten you about a few things. You won't find a better catch than my son. He's far beyond what any girl with your lowly background deserves. So let's work together. I want this wedding to take place soon, before that idiot son of mine has another chance to run off."

Maggie couldn't listen to any more. Eunice was out of control; the woman's desperation was starting to get a little scary. Maggie turned to the driver who stood silently beside the dining-room table, his hands folded in front of him. "Hamilton, you can take these all back out to the car," she murmured. Then she turned to Eunice, drawing a deep breath, her knuckles going white on the doorknob. "I'm not going to marry Colin," she said.

Eunice's eyes went wide and her mouth fell open. Then, with a dramatic groan, she pressed her palm to her chest and stumbled backward. "You can't be serious."

Maggie's fingers gripped the edge of the door. "I'm dead serious. And I think you should leave now," she said.

"I will not, you ungrateful little snip! You can't just dump my son without a—"

"You forget, Eunice, that he's the one who dumped me. Now, please, leave. I've got to pack."

"Where do you think you're going?"

She rubbed her forehead. "Somewhere where I can think. Where I can sort out the mess that my life has become and make a plan for my future. I certainly can't do that here." With that, Maggie let go of the door and turned toward the bedroom. "You can see yourself out."

When she got to the bedroom, she dragged her suitcases out of the closet and began to toss clothes into them. She jumped at the sound of the door slamming shut, then smiled in relief. That was another problem she could check off her list. Now, what to pack? Since she wasn't sure where she was headed, she gathered a variety of warm-weather and cold-weather attire and filled the bags.

Finished with her packing, Maggie dragged her luggage to the door, then picked up the phone and called her assistant manager at the shop. Kim happily agreed to watch the store for the next few days and to schedule additional sales help if she needed it. Maggie knew the shop would be in good hands. And what difference did it make anyway? In two more months, there wouldn't be a shop to worry about! A few lost sales here and there wouldn't have much impact in the grand scheme of life.

Minutes later, Maggie was speeding west on the Kennedy in her minivan, heading toward the airport. She'd hop a plane to someplace warm, she didn't care where or how far or how much a ticket cost, just as long as she could get away from Chicago. She wondered what the weather was like in Albania, wondered whether Luke would be basking beneath a warm sun or shivering in a rain-soaked tent.

A smile curled her lips as she thought about a warm destination, a beautiful Greek island, with soft Mediterranean breezes and water so blue it hurt the eyes. She'd lie beneath the sun, soaking up the warmth until it turned her skin to gold. And she'd splash in the water, washing away all the troubles of the past few days.

But as she spun out the fantasy, another character appeared at her side, a tall, handsome man with pale blue eyes and thick dark hair. They would be perfect strangers, the only Americans in some picturesque village. She would encounter some problem and he would come to her aid, at ease with the local customs and language. And the moment their eyes met, they'd become aware of an overwhelming passion, a passion they couldn't deny.

She saw them together, on the beach, in a beautiful villa, beside a pool. She'd touch him the same way she had that night in Colin's apartment, her fingers skimming along the hard muscle and smooth skin of his chest. And he'd kiss her, the way he had on her front steps, a kiss filled with passion and need. The fantasy built with every mile that passed, the images so vivid she couldn't help savoring each one individually.

When the signs for O'Hare appeared overhead, she ignored them and kept driving, first west and then north, unwilling to call an end to the daydream. As she drove, her mind was blissfully occupied with creating an ideal fantasy. First, she changed the setting and then the way they met and, finally, perfected the love scene until every element was so real she almost felt as if she'd experienced it herself.

By the time she finished her final and most erotic adventure, Maggie realized she'd been driving for nearly six hours, stopping only for gas and a chance to stretch her legs. A light snow had started to fall, the flakes hitting her windshield and swirling on the road in front of her.

She glanced over her road map, then slowed the van and pulled into a gas station, concerned the weather might get worse before it got better. When she put the van into park, she grabbed the map and stared at it, suddenly realizing where she was headed.

"Home," she murmured. "Oh, no, I'm going home." Back to Potter's Junction.

Tossing the map aside, Maggie slowly got out of the van. This is what she got for losing herself in a ridiculous fantasy! She hadn't been back to northern Wisconsin since her mother's funeral five years before and, even then, she couldn't bring herself to drive through Potter's Junction. The only pleasant memories she had of her hometown were with Luke—and she was supposed to be forgetting him!

Just as she decided to turn the van around and head in the opposite direction, the snowflakes began to fall in earnest, a nearly impenetrable wall of white, obscuring visibility. Maggie turned her face up to the sky. "What am I doing here?"

With a soft curse, she got into the van. She had no choice but to stay. Driving on the narrow highways was dangerous in the midst of a snowstorm, and the towns were few and far between. She'd have to find a room for the night and start back tomorrow.

POTTER'S JUNCTION WAS QUIET as she drove through town, the falling snow the only thing moving in the midafternoon light. She caught sight of familiar landmarks and was surprised to see new buildings in places that had been occupied by old haunts. In the summertime, Potter's Junction filled with tourists drawn to the quaint shops and nearby lakes. But in the winter, the town went into a peaceful hibernation, with only the whine of an occasional snowmobile splitting the cold, crisp air.

Many of the best motels and resorts were closed for the season, leaving her only a few choices. She finally stopped at the While-A-Way Lodge on the northern edge of town, a motley collection of faux log cabins. Maggie was familiar with the place as it was the spot where her mother met her fourth husband, a door-to-door encyclopedia salesman.

She parked the van, then walked to the manager's office. It was empty, so she rang the little bell on the desk and waited. "Hello," she called.

An elderly man wandered out from the back, his reading glasses perched on the end of his nose. He stared at her for a long time, his lower lip stuck out in a pensive expression. "You're Maggie Kelley," he said.

Maggie blinked, caught completely off guard. "Do I know you?"

"Naw. But I knew yer mother. Knew you, too, when you were just a skinny little thing." He tipped his chin up and examined her through the half lenses of his glasses. "You look just like Marlene, when she was younger. Though you turned out prettier than I would have expected. You filled out real nice."

"You knew my mother?" Maggie asked, wincing inwardly. But then, everyone in Potter's Junction knew Marlene Kelley. She'd been a legend in her own time.

The old man chuckled. "She was a little spitfire, that girl. Went to high school with her, I did. Every boy in the school had a crush on her. The prettiest girl in the county, she was."

Maggie frowned. She had expected some sordid story about one of her mother's love affairs, not a pleasant remembrance from an old acquaintance. "I—I need a room," Maggie said.

The manager shoved a card out in front of her and, after she filled it out, he carefully read the information she provided.

"Chicago, eh? You ever meet up with Luke Fitzpatrick down there? He's some big-time reporter. He's from Potter's Junction, too."

Maggie nodded and forced a smile. "Yes, I know. We're...acquainted." She wasn't about to pass along the fact that she'd spent the past six hours fantasizing about him.

"We get a lot of folks up here from Illinois, but not in the wintertime. You must be here for the festival. The First Annual Potter's Junction Millennium Festival. Special events every day and night for the rest of the week down at Fireman's Park. There's skating and ice fishing and hockey. And we've got the Snow Ball at the pavilion. That's a dance. I've got tickets for all the events. Interested?"

"Can I just have my key?" Maggie asked. "I won't be staying long."

The old man slid the key across the desk. "No smoking in the cabin, keep your shoes off the bedspread and don't open your door after ten at night. We get lots of snowmobilers stayin' here and they get a little boisterous. Sometimes they wander into the wrong cabins."

Maggie nodded, snatched her key and walked out the door. She grabbed her luggage from the van and dragged it to her cabin, skidding on the inch of fresh snow that had fallen since she'd arrived. Once her luggage was inside, she flopped down on the creaky bed. Now that she'd decided to stay for the night, she wasn't sure what to do.

"I'm hungry," she said, staring up at the ceiling. "And I'm tired."

In that instant, Maggie realized she hadn't slept more than a few hours in the past two nights. And she hadn't had anything to eat all day. First, she'd call Kim and let her know where she was. Then she'd wander out and try to find a quick dinner. After that, she'd crawl into bed and sleep for the next ten or twelve hours.

"At least I've finally got a plan," Maggie murmured, reaching for the phone. As she dialed the shop, her thoughts drifted back to Luke. By now, he was probably halfway to Albania.

Maggie had hoped that distance between them would put everything back on the right track. But now that he was half a world away, all she felt was an acute loneliness, a haze of melancholy that could only be eased by fantasies of him. Every time she allowed her thoughts to wander, they wandered to memories of his mouth on hers, of his strong fingers and his seductive voice, the feel of his skin beneath her palms.

Maggie groaned softly as the phone on the other end of the line rang.

"Clark Street Florists, Kim speaking."

"Hi, Kim. It's Maggie."

"Oh, Maggie, I'm so glad you called!"

Maggie sat up in bed, reacting to the panic she heard in her assistant manager's voice. "What is it? Is the power off again? I want you to unplug the coolers. Those compressors are almost brand new and if there's a power surge, they'll—"

"Everything is fine," Kim interrupted. "The power hasn't gone out again, the security system is working fine and we've had a decent day of sales."

"Then what is it? What's wrong?"

"It's Luke Fitzpatrick."

"Luke?" This time Maggie felt her own flood of panic tightening her throat and cutting off her air supply. "What is it? Is he all right? Is it his plane?" Awful visions raced through her mind of twisted metal on an Albanian mountainside.

"His plane?"

"He's on his way to Albania. Did his—"

"He's definitely not on his way to Albania. He's here in Chicago and he's been looking for you. He said he called your house and you didn't answer, then he went over and you weren't home. He stopped here and I told him you were gone, but you were planning to call in. What are you doing in Vegas?"

"I'm not in Las Vegas."

"Luke thought that's where you might be going. He thought you were going after Colin."

Maggie sighed. Their talk at the ice rink obviously hadn't done much good. Luke was still afraid she couldn't run her own life. "I'll call him," she finally said. "And I'll be back tomorrow afternoon, if the weather doesn't get too bad." She gave Kim the number for her cabin at the While-A-Way, then hung up.

But she couldn't bring herself to call Luke. It served him right to think that she'd gone after her fiancé. Let him worry, Maggie mused. Maybe he'd learn to quit butting into her business! Still, she couldn't help but feel flattered that he was so concerned.

He'd canceled his trip to Albania—for the third time, by her count. If there was one thing she did know about Luke Fitzpatrick, he never passed up a juicy assignment. Unless…

Her thoughts flashed back to her recent fantasies and she altered the scenario to fit a Chicago setting. Of course, there couldn't be any half-naked bodies since it was winter, but she could work with her limitations. She tried various locations first—his apartment, her coach house, a suite at the Drake Hotel, a shadowy corner in the produce aisle of her local grocery—

The phone jangled, startling her out of her reverie. Maggie rolled over to pick it up. "Stop thinking about him in that way," she muttered. Alone with her thoughts, it was hard to quit speculating about what might happen given the proper set of circumstances.

"Maggie?"

She expected to hear Kim's voice on the other end of the line. But as if he'd been reading her thoughts across the miles, Luke Fitzpatrick had managed to track her down.

Her throat convulsed and she coughed softly. "H-hi, Luke," she said, sitting up on the edge of the bed. "Kim told me you called the shop."

"Three times," he said, irritation evident in his voice. "Where the hell are you?"

"I'm not in Vegas, I can tell you that. I'm at the While-A-Way Lodge in Potter's Junction."

A long silence greeted her revelation, then a sharp laugh. "You're at the While-A-Way? That place with the twenty-foot-high deer in the parking lot."

"That's the place," Maggie said. "But the deer is gone. Now there's a big carved bear with a fish in its mouth."

"What the hell are you doing there?"

"I don't know," Maggie said. "I got in the van intending to go to O'Hare. I needed to get away, go someplace warm. And then the car just kept driving north and I ended up here." She left out the part about the six-hour fantasy. "I'll probably head back tomorrow if the weather gets better."

"Maybe you should stay," Luke suggested. "Take

some time. I don't want you driving if the roads are bad."

Maggie smiled at the gentle concern in his voice. "Maybe you're right. I'll think about it."

He paused for a long moment. "Well, I'll let you go then. I've got to run. My flight leaves in three hours. I'll call you when I get back from Albania. Sleep tight, Maggie, and stay safe."

"You, too," Maggie said, reluctant to let him go.

"I love you."

And then he was gone, the line going silent. Maggie held the phone clutched in her hand, staring at it in puzzlement. Had she really heard what she thought she'd heard? Hesitantly, she dropped the receiver in the cradle, then flopped down in the bed.

His words kept echoing in her head. What exactly did he mean? He'd never come right out and said he loved her, not in all the years they'd known each other. It had always been implied, but never said out loud. They loved each other like siblings. But why had he chosen now to tell her?

She stared at the ceiling, her gaze fixed on a water stain that looked like a duck. This was not what she needed right now! She had left Chicago to sort out her feelings and Luke had thrown just one more wrench into the works.

"He loves me like a sister," she murmured. "That's all he meant. And you are sick, sick, sick to think anything else."

In truth, all these fantasies she'd been formulating weren't a sign of a stable emotional state. Good grief, she'd been engaged to another man until a few days ago. Colin was barely out of her life before she had replaced a living, breathing fiancé with some dreamy vision of the perfect lover. And the fact that this dream guy had the face and the body of Luke Fitzpatrick was even worse!

Still, a secret part of her soul wanted his words to have a different meaning. Maggie could only wonder what it might be like to be loved by Luke Fitzpatrick, in the way a man loves a woman. And though she knew love might destroy everything they had between them, that didn't stop her from wanting just a tiny taste of that.

She threw her arm over her eyes and sighed. There had to be a way to put these dangerous feelings aside. But until she found the answer, she'd be smart to stay as far away from Luke Fitzpatrick as she could.

LUKE STOOD at the door of cabin seven at the While-A-Way Lodge. The sun was just beginning to rise in the eastern sky and the snow that had fallen all night now drifted on brisk winds. The drive north had been treacherous, but his Blazer had handled the trip without a major mishap, though it had taken nearly twice as long to get to Potter's Junction as it would have in the summer.

He wouldn't have had to make the drive if he hadn't made such a mess of everything on the phone last night. He'd only had the best intentions when he'd called her, anxious to make sure she was all right, curious to know if she'd gone looking for Colin. And the conversation had been pretty innocent, right up until the moment he hung up. Geez, what had gotten into him, telling Maggie he loved her?

The words had just come out without him even thinking. Not that he didn't mean what he'd said, but he certainly couldn't have meant it in a romantic way. And right now, their relationship was on such shaky ground, he didn't want any misunderstandings.

Luke rubbed his eyes and brushed the snow out of his hair. He felt as if he'd spent the past few days doing nothing but damage control with Maggie. First, he'd tried to convince her not to marry Colin and he'd paid dearly for that. Then he'd kissed her and had to apologize twice before she forgave him. And now this.

Who knew what she thought of him after they hung up last night? Could she possibly believe he had romantic feelings toward her? Or had she simply taken it as a brotherly expression of his affection? Whatever she thought, he planned to straighten it out right away and get everything back on track before he finally took off for Albania.

Luke raised his hand to knock on the door, then drew away. So what was he going to tell her? What was his excuse for saying something so—spontaneous? He certainly couldn't blame this blunder on too much champagne. And he couldn't tell her it was just a natural expression of his feelings at the moment—even though it was. He'd have to go with the brotherly story, that was his best bet.

Luke rapped on the door, and waited for her to answer. But no one stirred inside the cabin. He knocked on the door again, this time with his fist.

"You have the wrong room." Maggie's voice was muffled by the door.

He knocked once more and waited.

"Go away!" she shouted. "I'm trying to sleep!"

"Maggie? Let me in. It's Luke."

A few seconds later, the door swung open and Maggie stood in the doorway, dressed in only a T-shirt that hung loosely on her slender frame, her long legs bare and undeniably sexy. She squinted up at him and pushed her rumpled hair from her eyes. The cold wind blew in around her and her teeth chattered, but she still continued to look at him in confusion.

"Maggie? Are you going to let me come in?"

She tilted her head, rubbing her arms with her hands. "What are you doing here? Aren't you supposed to be in Albania?"

Luke was hearing that question a lot lately. Though he'd had every intention of getting on that plane a few hours before, he just couldn't seem to do it. "Can we talk about this inside? It's freezing out here and you're going to catch a cold."

She stepped aside and let him pass, then swung the door shut behind him. With a soft moan, she hurried over to the bed and crawled beneath the covers, pulling them up to her chin. He stood in the middle of the room, so tempted to crawl right into bed beside her, yet certain that would be a mistake. Sharing a bed with Maggie wasn't what he'd come here for.

"What time is it?" she asked in a sleepy voice.

He glanced at his watch. "It's about 6:00 a.m."

She moaned and pressed her face into the pillow. "So are you going to tell me why you're here or are you just going to stand there?"

He crossed to the bed and sat down on the edge. He wanted to take her hand or touch her, but he couldn't. He wasn't sure how he'd react to the feel of her fingers in his. They were, after all, in a motel room, alone. And she looked awfully tempting in that T-shirt. A simple touch could turn into trouble. "About last night, on the phone. I—I wanted to explain—what I meant."

She looked up at him, her face still half hidden by the pillow. "You really don't have to. I know exactly what you meant."

"You do?"

Maggie nodded. "You meant love in a brotherly

way. Not love in a romantic way. You didn't have to drive here to tell me that."

Luke sighed and leaned back against the headboard, kicking his feet up onto the bed. That's what he should have meant. But now that *she* had put it into words, he wasn't so sure anymore. He certainly didn't feel like her brother. Yet he wasn't her lover. He was stuck somewhere in between, in a strange limbo that caused more confusion than it was worth.

He closed his eyes and drew a long breath. "Yeah," he said. "That's what I meant."

Maggie sighed. "You could have called," she murmured in a sleepy voice.

Luke slouched down a bit, then looked over at her. He fought the urge to kiss her, to press his lips to her forehead, to her closed eyes, to her upturned nose and soft mouth. To nuzzle his face in the warm curve of her neck and to inhale the scent of her hair. "I thought it was important. I didn't want you to think that— that—"

"That you loved me the other way a man might love a woman?"

"Um," he said. "I guess so."

She snuggled farther down into the warmth of the bed. "I didn't think that," she said. "Not for a single minute."

A long silence grew between them and, as Luke sat next to her, he listened to her breathing grow deep and even. He'd never had the opportunity to study her so freely and it was at that very moment that he realized something. There were times when he looked at Maggie and saw the girl that she had been. And other times when he noticed the woman she'd become. But now, he saw something much more. He saw a woman he cherished, a woman who was more than just a friend. And he also saw a woman who awakened his desire.

He pressed his lips to the tip of his finger, reached over and ran his fingertip along her cheek, barely skimming her silken skin. Her eyelids fluttered and a soft sigh slipped from her lips, but then she grew still again.

He'd slept in a lot of places, some more dangerous than others. But no matter where he'd been, he'd always kept a constant vigil, never resting so deeply that he might miss signs of impending trouble. Even when he was at home, in his own bed, he couldn't shake his battlefield instincts.

Yet as he lay here beside Maggie, Luke knew he was about to fall asleep in the most dangerous spot in the world. But here, he could close his eyes and dream, sleep more deeply than he had in years. His eyes began to get heavy and he closed them, intending to rest them for just a moment, before leaving to find a room of his own.

In the end, he drifted off, curled against her warm body and satisfied he'd put everything to rights—for the time being. The fact that he was falling in love with his best friend was still a problem. But that problem wasn't one that he was in any hurry to solve.

6

MAGGIE WASN'T SURE what woke her, whether it was the sound of deep, even breathing or the hiss of the windblown snow against the windows. She opened her eyes slowly, only to find her nose mere inches from Luke's. Her heart lurched and she fought the temptation to wriggle to the far edge of the bed. At the same moment, she tried to figure out how they'd ended up in bed together in the first place.

She vaguely remembered his arrival, letting him into her cabin and crawling back under the covers. After that, all she could recall was drifting back to sleep. Sometime in between then and now, Luke had curled up beside her, still dressed in his boots and jacket.

He had always told her he could sleep anywhere—airports, train stations, park benches. It had become a professional necessity, snatching a few winks whenever he could to fight off jet lag or time shifts or overwhelming exhaustion. But the last place she'd ever expected him to drift off was in her bed. Not that she didn't enjoy the experience, Maggie mused, her gaze skimming his face.

His breath was like a warm caress on her cheek and his hand rested on her hip in an oddly possessive manner. Somehow, their legs had become tangled together, twisted in the blankets. She sighed, an unfamiliar contentment washing over her. This must be how lovers felt, waking up the morning after a night of passion.

Safe and warm and satisfied. Except lovers usually didn't wear boots to bed—or three layers of clothing.

Lying here with Luke, she could actually imagine them as lovers. Luke was a passionate man, driven and intense, and Maggie knew those qualities would be there in his lovemaking. He had powerful needs and he stopped at nothing to see them satisfied. Just the thought of him turning his desire in her direction made her heart beat faster and the blood heat in her veins.

Her eyes slowly took in the details of his face, the dark eyebrows that arched so flawlessly, the impossibly thick lashes and his perfectly straight nose. His brow, usually furrowed in concentration, was smooth and his hair tumbled over his forehead in a boyish wave.

She'd never had the chance to study him at such close range, but now she reveled in the opportunity. He really was the most handsome man she'd ever known, though she wasn't sure why she hadn't realized it before. She'd always looked at him through a haze of childhood memories and hero worship. Why had it taken her so long to see him for what he really was—a flesh-and-blood man? She swallowed hard. An incredibly sexy man.

Maggie frowned and shifted her gaze to his lips. His chiseled mouth was his most intriguing feature, she mused. Probably because she'd experienced that mouth firsthand. She wondered how many women he'd kissed, then concluded he'd probably kissed more than she'd care to count.

He was a good kisser, though—so much more accomplished than Colin. Colin's kisses had always been rather perfunctory, as if he was simply fulfilling a bothersome responsibility to make Maggie feel wanted.

When Luke kissed her, she felt a connection, as if a wild current of passion passed between them.

He kissed better than any man she'd ever known, not that she'd known many. Men hadn't exactly been a commodity in Maggie's life. She'd had a few boyfriends and fewer lovers, but she'd never been able to give herself over completely to intimacy. In every relationship, including hers with Colin, she'd held a part of herself back, guarded a piece of her heart as if it were as precious as gold. Maybe it was self-preservation, a way to protect her heart from anything that might break it. Or maybe it was just in her nature to mistrust her emotions.

She felt an intimacy with Luke that she felt with no one else. Maggie could tell him anything without fear or regret. She trusted him completely. And she didn't have to hold back.

Maggie frowned. There was one thing she couldn't admit to Luke—her feelings for him had changed. She couldn't tell him she craved his touch and dreamed about his kisses. She couldn't confess that she was drawn to him in a purely physical way. And worst of all, she couldn't say that she feared she might never again be able to view him as just a friend.

A ragged breath slipped from her lips. How was she supposed to fight this? Common sense warned that to fall in love with Luke would be to risk a friendship it took a lifetime to build. And how could she know whether she was falling in love with the hero or the man?

After what had happened with Colin, maybe all she needed was a hero, someone to remind her she was worth caring about. Maybe that's all she wanted from Luke—reassurance. Isn't that what he'd always given her in the past? It could be so easy to mistake appreciation for love.

"That's it, then," Maggie whispered. She didn't really love Luke; she just needed him to get over this rough spot in her life. And when she could finally put her short-lived engagement behind her, she would realize that she and Luke were only friends.

But what did Luke want? He didn't seem to be satisfied with playing the hero anymore. At every turn, she caught him pushing the boundaries of their friendship, steering them both into more intimate territory. He was testing her defenses, advancing and retreating and advancing again, waiting for some sign from her.

Slowly, she drew her hand up and ran her finger along the line of his jaw, so lightly he didn't react. Rough stubble scraped her fingertip and she felt an overwhelming ache deep in her core. She wanted to touch him again and again, just like this. To simply reach out and make contact whenever she felt the urge, whenever she needed reassurance. To know he'd be there for her.

"What do *you* want?" she murmured, her words as soft as a sigh. "Why are you here?"

With trembling fingers, she placed her palm gently on his cheek and leaned forward. But before she could kiss him, his eyelids fluttered and she drew back. Frozen, her hand still resting on his cheek, Maggie waited for him to drift back to sleep, anxious to retrieve her hand.

Then his eyes opened. He stared at her for a long time, his gaze uncomprehending at first. Then he smiled, leaned toward her and brushed an exquisitely soft kiss across her mouth, his tongue lining the crease of her lips. Not a word passed between them, only a look that seemed to go on and on, spinning out around them. And then his eyes closed, and within seconds, he was asleep.

Maggie held her breath, secretly praying he would wake up again and pick up where he'd left off, willing him to open his eyes. But as she waited, she slowly realized she wasn't ready for more than a kiss. They were together, alone, in a motel room, with nothing to stop them from tossing aside common sense and propriety and moving on to more passionate matters.

Ten minutes later, she'd managed to extricate herself from the bed without waking him. She stood over Luke for a long time, watching him breathe in and out, marveling at how easily he slept, how comfortable he looked in her bed. She fought the temptation to crawl back in, to curl up beside his warm body and to wake him slowly with kisses of her own. In the end, Maggie turned and grabbed her clothes from a chair near the window.

She had to get out of the room before she gave in to temptation. "Lunch," Maggie murmured. "I'll get us both some lunch."

Maggie retreated to the bathroom, her feet cold on the tile floor. When she looked into the mirror, she groaned in dismay. Pale hair stuck up in errant spikes and tangled waves. Her mascara had smudged until she looked like a circus clown. Thank God, he'd gone back to sleep! Had he looked at her through lucid eyes, he might have wriggled out of bed himself. Frantically, she scrubbed yesterday's makeup from her face with the tiny bar of motel soap, then dragged a brush through her hair.

After she finished dressing, Maggie sneaked out of the bathroom and silently tugged on her boots and jacket, keeping one eye on Luke the entire time. It wouldn't do to wake him now. Wincing, she pulled the door open, only to be met by blinding white light.

The entire world glistened and glittered under freshly fallen snow. Maggie waded through a drift on her way out to her car. But the van was buried beneath nearly twelve inches of powder. She looked around the parking lot, then decided to take off on foot. If she remembered correctly, there was a diner not too far down the road.

As she strolled back into town, she looked at Potter's Junction through new eyes. She remembered the town as such a dismal place with dour inhabitants and run-down buildings. How odd that everything looked so different now. The trees were coated with snow, turning the streets into a fairyland. The houses were prettier, the people friendlier. Children played in the snow and dogs raced around their feet, barking and jumping.

Everything was so bright and sunny—and happy. Could this be the same town she had come to despise so many years ago? The place she had run from without a glance back? Maybe everything looked so wonderful because she was truly happy.

Maggie stopped in the middle of the sidewalk and pondered that notion for a moment. "What do I have to be happy about?" she murmured. "My fiancé ran off with my best girlfriend. In a couple of months, I'll lose the business I spent years building. And I'm developing a serious case of lust for a man I consider a dear friend. And for the first time in my life, I don't have a plan." To an objective viewer, her life would look like a train wreck.

Luke had told her he loved her—even though he might not have meant it in the way she wanted. And they'd kissed again—even though he probably didn't remember it. And he'd fallen asleep in her bed—even though he was fully clothed. But on the whole, Maggie still managed to have a more positive outlook today than she'd had yesterday.

Maybe coming to Potter's Junction hadn't been such a bad idea. As she walked down the street, she realized she had more to her past than Luke. Though most of her memories outside of him were difficult, they were still her memories. And in a way, her life in Potter's Junction had made her into the person she was today. A person who could survive a broken engagement and a friend's betrayal and a failed business and go on with her life.

"I *am* happy," she said, drawing a deep breath of the crisp, fresh air. Maggie laughed, then held up her arms and fell into the pristine snow next to the sidewalk. Scissoring her arms and legs, she made a snow angel the way she'd done when she was a little girl. Three children scampered up beside her and dropped into the snow beside her, adding baby angels to the tableau.

As she lay staring up at the brilliant blue sky through the snow-kissed trees, Maggie remembered her New Year's resolution: "I will marry Colin Spencer and be deliriously happy."

There wasn't any chance she'd be walking down the aisle with Colin, but right here, right now, Maggie truly believed she could be deliriously happy in the new millennium. And she suspected her happiness depended on the man sleeping in her cabin at the While-A-Way Lodge.

LUKE STOOD under the feeble spray of a barely warm shower, letting the water run down his back. He braced his hands on the tile wall and closed his eyes. He hadn't expected to wake up alone, but when he looked at his watch he wasn't surprised. It was nearly noon and sunlight filled the little motel room, warming the chill out of the air. He'd slept a good six hours without waking, a solid night's sleep in his book.

Maggie was nowhere to be found, but her van was still buried by snow in the lot, so Luke assumed she'd be back sooner or later. She'd come all this way to Potter's Junction for a reason, though he wasn't sure what it was. Maggie hadn't been back since she'd left eleven years ago. Her mother's funeral had taken place in a nearby town and though they'd traveled to northern Wisconsin together for the service, Maggie had refused even to drive through Potter's Junction.

Luke knew she struggled with the memories from her childhood, but what had she hoped to gain by driving here and back in less than twenty-four hours? Had she come here looking for answers? Or was she just trying to escape all the questions in Chicago?

He raked his hands through his wet hair and rubbed the rough stubble on his face. In truth, Luke wasn't all that anxious for Maggie to return—not until he'd sorted a few things out first. He still hadn't told her that he'd heard from her runaway fiancé, that Colin fully intended to come back to Chicago and reclaim what he thought was still his.

Why was he waiting? Was it because he really didn't believe Colin was the right man for Maggie, that she might go back to her runaway fiancé? Or did Luke have his own designs on Maggie Kelley?

It was getting nearly impossible to deny his feelings. Since the moment he had learned of her engagement, time had begun to slip through his fingers. In truth, that's why he had delayed the Albania assignment, out of fear that he'd return to learn he had lost Maggie for good. They couldn't go on living in this limbo between friendship and desire. Sooner or later they'd both need to take a step one way or the other. He just didn't want it to be the wrong step.

"What do you want, Fitzpatrick? Make up your mind."

Luke flipped off the water, then grabbed a towel from the rack, wrapped it around his waist and stepped from the shower. Steam clouded the mirror and he wiped it off with his hand, then stared at his reflection.

He wanted Maggie. Even though he knew he had nothing to offer her, he still wanted her. He couldn't be the husband she needed, the guy with the nine-to-five and the fat paycheck. He wouldn't be around to help raise the kids or mow the lawn or even be home to take his wife out for their anniversary once a year.

Maggie needed so much more than he could give her. But what about what *he* needed? Didn't he deserve a little consideration as well? Luke adjusted the towel around his waist and walked out of the bathroom. "You're being selfish, Fitzpatrick," he muttered. "Think about Maggie."

He picked up the clothes he wore yesterday, then realized his bag was outside in the truck. He slipped his bare feet into boots and grabbed his jacket, intending to make a quick run to the truck, but as he reached for the door, it opened in front of him.

Maggie looked up as she stepped inside, then stopped short, a bundle of bags in her arms. "You're awake," she said, her gaze flitting from his face to his naked chest to the damp towel slung low around his hips. He watched as a pretty blush stained her cheeks. She ducked her head as she stepped past him to place the bags on the bed.

"I—I brought some lunch," she said. Glancing over

her shoulder, she forced a smile. "Were you planning to go out like that?"

"Just to my truck," Luke replied. "I left my bag out there."

"Oh, I can get it," she offered, moving toward the open door.

He closed it, then shook his head. "I'll go out later."

She shrugged then went back to the bed and began to pick through the bags. The smell of cheeseburgers bloomed in the air and Luke realized he hadn't eaten since a few hours before he'd left Chicago. He dropped his jacket on the floor, kicked off his boots and crossed to the bed. Wide-eyed, Maggie handed him a burger, which he quickly unwrapped.

"A-aren't you cold?" she asked, glancing at him nervously.

Luke shook his head and looked around the room. "I've lived in conditions a lot worse than the While-A-Way Lodge," he replied. "This place has heat and plumbing. A real roof. It's positively luxurious. And the bed was pretty comfortable, too."

She swallowed, then snatched up a can of soda and took a long drink. It was then he realized his state of undress was making her uneasy. He smiled inwardly. She had denied any attraction between them so vehemently he had almost started to believe she felt nothing for him. But now, watching her gaze flit across his naked chest, her words turning breathless and her movements becoming awkward, Luke knew the truth.

Maggie's attraction to him was as powerful as his toward her. She was just better at hiding her desire than he had been. But here, alone with him, she couldn't deny it for long. All he'd have to do would be to give her a little push, test her resolve. He wondered how she would react if he tossed aside his cheeseburger and his towel, and proceeded to ravish her, right here on the squeaky motel bed.

"So," she said, interrupting his thoughts, "when are you going back?"

Luke shrugged. "Whenever you are. I'll just follow you. We should probably get on the road before long. I'd like to get to Madison by late afternoon, so you won't have to drive too far in the dark."

"I've decided to stay for a while," Maggie said. She pulled a brochure from her jacket pocket. "There's a craft fair today and tomorrow and an ice sculpture contest and this isn't such a bad place to celebrate the new millennium."

"Then I'll stay," Luke said, grabbing a handful of fries and popping a few in his mouth.

She followed suit, then coughed softly when her food went down the wrong way. "Here?"

"Why not? I need a break. I haven't had a vacation in ages. And we'll have a chance to spend some time together, have some fun, see the old hometown. I don't need to leave for Albania until the weekend."

"I—I meant, here," Maggie said. "In this cabin. My cabin."

Luke grinned and took a sip of chocolate malt. "What's wrong?" he teased. "Was I hogging the bed? I thought we both slept pretty well. I guess we're compatible in bed, too."

She took another bite of burger, a blush darkening her already rosy cheeks. "This—this isn't a joke," she said in a strangled voice, her mouth still half-full. "We used to be friends and now—now I don't know what we are." She set her food down and pressed her palms into her thighs. "This is very confusing."

She looked so lost, bewildered by all that had passed between them. Luke couldn't help feeling a bit guilty about his part in her growing anxiety. He hadn't really made his motives clear. And he would have, if he'd known what his motives were himself. One minute, Maggie was the object of his desire, the next minute, his oldest and dearest friend.

"What do you want us to be?" he asked, reaching out to grab her hand. Her fingers were so slender against his palm, as if they would break if he gripped her hand too hard. He knew her features so well, down to the delicate pink of her fingernails. Every detail had been imprinted in his mind long ago, scored so deeply he would be able to recognize Maggie by touch alone. How many men could claim to know their own wives as well as he knew Maggie?

"I—I want things to go back to the way they were," she murmured. "I want you to wear clothes when we're together and I don't want you to kiss me anymore. We can't sleep in the same bed. I—I want us to be friends again."

"We are friends," Luke said softly. "Does that mean we can't be more?"

"No!" Maggie cried. "It would spoil everything. We might fall in love and then we'd start to fight and then you'd leave and I'd never see you again. Just like—"

"Just like your mother and all her husbands?"

"No!" She frowned. "Yes, maybe." Maggie drew a ragged breath. "I've seen how easy it is to fall in and out of love. It happens just like that," she said, snapping her fingers. "And there's nothing a person can do to stop it."

"And what about Colin?"

"I never loved Colin," Maggie said in a frustrated tone. As soon as the words were out of her mouth, she pressed her fingers to her lips as if she wanted to take them right back.

"You were going to marry him," Luke said, caught off guard by her admission. "And you didn't love him?"

"I didn't mean that." She grabbed an empty bag and folded it neatly. "Of course I loved him."

Maggie was lying. He could see it in her eyes. "That's not what you said."

She stared down at her hands for a long time, then drew a deep breath. "That's why I was going to marry him," she explained in a voice void of emotion. "Because, deep down, I knew I didn't love him. I guess I figured if I didn't love him and he left me, then it couldn't possibly hurt. That was all part of the plan."

Luke shook his head. He should have known. He'd always been able to read Maggie, to discern her deepest feelings, but they'd been together so little this past year that he'd lost his touch. Good God, she'd almost married a man she didn't love! "But did it hurt?"

"It was…embarrassing," Maggie said. "That's all."

Luke reached out and placed his palm on her flushed cheek. Then, unable to stop himself, he leaned over and touched his lips to hers. "I'm sorry," he murmured.

Hesitantly, she drew back, but just enough to look up into his eyes. "You shouldn't kiss me," Maggie insisted, her breath soft on his cheek. "Friends don't kiss—at least, not like that."

"And what if I don't want to be friends?"

Her eyes went wide and he could see hurt in their green depths. "You—you don't want to—"

He cursed silently. "I still want to be friends. But what if I want more?"

"More?"

He leaned forward again and kissed her, this time lingering for a moment longer. Her fingers fluttered to his chest and she pressed her palms against his naked skin. The warmth from her fingers seeped into his blood and began to pool in his lap. Luke groaned and deepened the kiss, unable to stop himself.

The taste of her was like a drug, powerful and addictive. He slipped his hand to her nape and gently eased her back into the mattress. She stiffened beneath him, then pressed her hands against his chest. Dazed by desire, Luke reluctantly drew away.

Maggie struggled from the bed, then stood beside him, her arms crossed over her chest, her face flushed. "Why did you come here? Why aren't you on your way to Albania? Don't you have a war to get to?"

Luke ran his hand through his hair. In all honesty, he wasn't sure why he'd come. He could have explained the "I love you" with another phone call, so it wasn't that. And he certainly didn't enjoy driving twelve hours through a raging blizzard. "I came because I wanted to," he finally said. *I came because I wanted you.*

"I think you should get your own cabin if you plan to stay. I—I'll go make arrangements with the manager while you get dressed."

Luke studied her for a long moment. She looked as if she wanted to be anyplace but here, in this cabin, with him. Was she worried he might kiss her again, that things between them might become more than she could handle? Or was Maggie simply intent on preserving their friendship—as shaky as it had become?

He kept returning to the kiss they'd shared that night on her front porch. He'd sensed passion there, a passion he felt compelled to explore. Luke Fitzpatrick never let a story go until he had all the facts, until he'd plumbed all the nuances, and those qualities stood him in good stead now. He wasn't going to leave Maggie

alone until he knew exactly how she felt about him—
and how he felt about her.

"Would you rather I went back to Chicago?" he
asked.

Maggie drew a deep breath. "I'm just not sure what
you're doing here. I thought we decided to forget what
happened that night at my house."

"It's forgotten," he said. "I've moved on."

"To telling me you love me? To sleeping in my bed?
To—to prancing around half-naked in my cabin?"

He laughed. "I do love you. I was tired. And I don't
prance." With a sigh, he stood up, grabbed his jeans
and headed toward the bathroom. "I better get
dressed." His towel had loosened, but he didn't bother
to adjust it. It slipped from his waist just as he reached
the bathroom door. He grabbed it and tossed it over his
shoulder, giving her an eyeful.

When he closed the door behind him, Luke could
only imagine the blush that stained her cheeks now.
He didn't care. It was time to shake things up. He was
tired of being Maggie's friend, the guy with the honorable intentions, the knight in shining armor. He
wanted more.

He was only in the bathroom for a few moments,
long enough to throw aside the towel and pull on his
jeans. A soft rap sounded on the door and with a grin,
Luke pulled it open. Maggie stood there, her hands
clenched in front of her. She risked a glance up at him
and met his gaze without flinching.

"I love you, too," she said. "I just wanted you to
know that."

"And what does that mean?" he asked, his gaze fixing on her lush lips, his mind wandering to the taste of
her kisses.

"It means you're very important to me," she said.

"Just like I'm important to you. We're friends and we care about each other. And I don't want that to change."

With that, she spun on her heel and walked to the door. A cold draft blew through the room as she stepped outside. He stood there, his shoulder braced against the doorjamb, staring at the closed door.

"So we love each other," he muttered. Luke drew a deep breath and rubbed his palm over his chest. "What the hell am I supposed to do now?"

"WHERE ARE WE GOING?" Maggie asked, trying to keep up with Luke's long gait. She had returned to the room to find him dressed and ready to go. After what she'd said to him, she had almost dreaded going back. But she'd spoken her mind—Maggie did love Luke as much as he loved her, and in exactly the same way he loved her. It seemed, though, that neither of them knew exactly what way that was—passionate or platonic.

Now that she'd gotten him his own cabin at the While-A-Way, at least she would have the time and space to figure it all out. And she wouldn't have to risk another tantalizing look at his naked backside. The image stuck in her mind, replaying over and over again until she was certain he had the most incredible body in the history of mankind—at least from the rear.

While Maggie had been in the motel office, Luke had looked over the brochure she'd brought back and agreed it would be fun to take in the Potter's Junction millennium festivities. In truth, she was grateful they'd both find something else to occupy their minds and bodies. Idle time was a ticket to trouble with Luke Fitzpatrick.

Though Maggie was bothered by the desire that kept

popping up between them, Luke seemed completely at ease. Maybe that was just a characteristic of his sex. Physical intimacy wasn't a cerebral thing to a man. It was all about the body, action and reaction. She was the one who couldn't shut down her brain and enjoy the moment. Whenever he touched her, her mind began to whirl and her thoughts turned chaotic as she tried to reason out what was happening between them.

As they walked through the parking lot, Maggie drew a long breath of crisp air and her mind cleared. She'd have fun today and, along the way, she and Luke would rebuild their shaky friendship. What better place to do that but in Potter's Junction?

They set off on foot as they always had, with no plan in mind, no destination decided. Hand in hand, they wandered through the tiny downtown area and marveled at the festive atmosphere. Ice sculptures lined the sidewalks and they cast their votes for their favorites at the tourist office. Local craftsmen had set up tents and tables and were selling everything from carved loons to leather moccasins to fishing lures.

Tourists who had ventured north for the New Year's celebration wandered the streets, peering into shop windows, entranced by the quaint north-woods items offered for sale. Luke bought Maggie a hot-spiced cider to sip as they strolled and, gradually, they settled into the easy familiarity that had marked their friendship from the very first days.

They couldn't have been further from all the glitz and glamour of Chicago's millennium celebrations. In truth, Maggie was starting to enjoy the peaceful atmosphere of her hometown, a town she'd been reluctant to claim. The connection to her past—a connection that, until now, she'd only felt with Luke—was growing stronger here in Potter's Junction. And here was so far away from there—from the memories of Chicago and Colin Spencer.

"Look," Luke said, pointing to a sign. "That's what we're going to do today."

"What?" Maggie said as Luke grabbed her hand and pulled her along before she could read the sign.

"Down at the lake," he murmured. "Fireman's Park. I wonder if we need a license."

She stopped and turned to him. "We're going to do something that requires a license?" Maggie frowned. "I'm not sure I like the sound of that."

"You'll love it. I promise," he reassured her. "It's just the right thing for old friends to do."

By the time they reached the lake, a small crowd had gathered near the bandstand in Fireman's Park. Luke and Maggie stood at the back of the group and listened to an elderly man who stood on top of a milk crate. Her attention wandered and she glanced at the bearded gentleman next to her. Whatever Luke had planned for them, Maggie realized they were woefully underdressed.

The rest of the people—both men and women—in the group were garbed from head to toe in snowmobile suits of a variety of unattractive colors, from fluorescent orange to muddy khaki to camouflage. Maggie had her down jacket and a pair of boots made for the stylish Chicago winters, fashionable but barely functional. She listened with half an ear to a long explanation about some contest, but it was only when the old man began to talk about bait and lures that she realized Luke intended for them to fish!

After all the rules were confirmed, Luke purchased a fishing license for them both at a table set up on the bandstand. The contest chairman pointed out a tiny shack near the middle of the ice, informing them that it was stocked with all the equipment and bait needed for the amateur fisherman and out-of-town visitor, compliments of the local sportsman's club.

Luke thanked the man and they set off across the ice, Maggie wary of cracks and holes and the dark water beneath her feet. "I don't think I like this," she muttered.

"You haven't even tried it yet."

"But how are we going to get at the fish?" she asked. "There's a foot of ice between us and them."

Luke pointed to the ramshackle shanty out on the ice. "They've already cut a hole for us inside that shelter. We just drop in our line and wait."

By the time they settled into the shed on the ice, Maggie was half-frozen and completely miserable. Luke handed her a short little fishing pole and patted the upside-down milk crate next to him. "Sit," he said. "I'll bait your hook."

She shivered as she watched him attach a small fish to the end of her line and drop it into the hole. A cork bobbed on the surface. "Why are we here?" Maggie said. "Neither one of us knows anything about ice fishing."

"How hard can it be?" Luke said with a grin. "Besides, you said no more kissing." He glanced around. "This is the only place you're going to be safe, Maggie. We're both fully clothed, there's not a bed in sight. And I've always heard fishing fosters good conversation. We'll just sit out here and talk, like old friends." He glanced up. "That's what you want, isn't it?"

They sat silently for a long time, both of them staring at the corks attached to their lines. As far as Maggie was concerned, sitting on a milk crate in a tiny hut in the middle of a frozen lake was the last place she wanted to have a long conversation. She much preferred coffee shops and wine bars, anyplace with heat. Her teeth began to chatter and she stomped her feet on the ice to restore circulation.

"So, wh-what should we t-talk about?" she asked.

"You're not supposed to plan the conversation," Luke replied. "It just happens."

"Well, while we're waiting for it to happen, I'm slowly slipping into hypothermia. If you want me to respond, you better start talking."

Luke continued to stare into the water, gently jiggling his rod. Maggie couldn't imagine that two people without any fishing experience could even hook a fish, much less catch a winning entry. Ice fishing was an exercise in subzero futility, as was this attempt at serious conversation.

"Are you ever curious?" Luke asked.

Maggie frowned. "Curious about what? Whether there actually are fish alive beneath this ice? Or what mental disease overtook your mind when you decided we should ice-fish?"

"Have you ever been curious about us?" he clarified. "What it would be like."

Maggie sucked in a sharp breath, the cold hurting her chest. "What?"

He glanced up. "You and me. Together. Haven't you ever thought about it? It's an easy question. Yes or no."

She let her breath out and it clouded around her face. "No," she lied.

"What about New Year's Eve, when you kissed me on your front porch? Were you curious then?"

"No!" Maggie cried. "I was upset and—and distraught. I was confused."

"And curious," Luke added. "When you kissed me that second time. That was definitely curiosity."

"*You* kissed *me* the second time." Maggie shoved her

fishing pole into his hands and stood up, ready to stalk away. But she was in the middle of the lake, a long cold walk from shore. And all she could think about was plunging through the ice with no one at her side to pull her out.

"All right," she finally said, turning to him. "I have been curious. But that doesn't mean I have to appease my curiosity. You're a man, I'm a woman. It's only natural. But I can control my curiosity."

He nodded, then went back to his fishing. Maggie stared at him for a long moment. "Is that it?" she asked.

"Yeah, that's it. Is there anything you'd like to ask?"

She wanted to ask if he'd let the towel slip off his hips on purpose. Or if he remembered kissing her in his dreams. Maggie wanted to know if touching her the way he had made his blood run hot and his heart beat faster.

"If I had known how much trouble kissing you would cause, I never would have done it," Maggie muttered, sitting down beside him. "It was a stupid mistake."

"That has yet to be seen," Luke said in a soft voice. A smile curled the corners of his mouth and he held out her pole. "I think you've got a bite."

"A bite of what?" Maggie asked.

He chuckled. "There's a fish on your line."

Maggie fumbled with the pole and Luke helped her operate the reel. "Oh, I've got a fish? I've got a fish!" Slowly, she wound in the line, her hands trembling, until a fish popped out of the hole and flopped onto the ice. Maggie looked to Luke for help. "Now what?"

"I think that's a bluegill. Looks like a good size. It might win a prize, but we'll have to take it back and get it measured."

"But won't it die if it stays out of the water that long?"

"Yeah. But you can't prove you caught a winner if you throw it back. Then everyone would claim they caught a three-foot bass."

"Put it back," Maggie demanded, bending over to examine the gasping bluegill. "How could they hold a contest that advocates killing fish?"

Luke grabbed the fish and carefully removed the hook from its mouth, then gently lowered it into the water. He chuckled as he wiped his hands on his jeans. "You're just too softhearted for fishing," he said. "You've got to toughen up."

Their eyes met and, for a long time, she couldn't look away. Something in his gaze touched her heart, a tenderness she'd never noticed before. A smile quirked the corners of his mouth and he shook his head.

"No, that's wrong," he said, pushing her pole back into her hands. "Don't change. You've always had a kind heart, Maggie. I can't count how many injured birds and starving squirrels I helped you rescue over the years."

Maggie busied herself with reeling in her line. She wanted to lean toward him and take his hand, to close her eyes and anticipate the warm touch of his mouth on hers. Kissing him seemed like the only right thing to do at the moment. "You were the only hero I knew," Maggie said softly. "There was no one else to call."

They went back to fishing, a gentle conversation growing between them. They didn't talk of curiosity and declarations of love. Or frantic hands and damp towels that slipped off on the way to the bathroom. Instead, they discussed inconsequential things, things that friends found fascinating. And when they finally walked off the ice, both of them nearly frozen to the bone, Maggie knew nothing could ever come between them—not lust or love or long miles.

No matter what happened, at least they would always be friends.

7

"IT HASN'T CHANGED much, has it?"

Luke stood in front of the office of the *Lake Country Register*, staring through the plate-glass window that reflected the bright noonday sun. He gave Maggie's hand a squeeze. "It looks just like it did when I delivered newspapers as a kid."

This is where his life first intersected with journalism, his attention captured by a hand-lettered sign pasted in the front window. He'd been riding his bike past on the way home from school and stopped in to apply. By the next morning, he'd been issued the canvas bags for the back fender and a list of subscribers.

He smiled as he remembered how long it had taken him to aim and throw the rolled-up papers accurately. For the first few weeks, Maggie had followed him on her bike, running back and forth between the sidewalk and the house to correct his mistakes. She'd happily tagged along, even after he'd perfected his accuracy, content to sit with him and fold papers or help him settle his accounts every month.

"You should go in," Maggie said. "I'm sure Mr. Winslow would be happy to see you."

Luke glanced at her. "Come in with me."

She shook her head. "I want to browse through that antique store down the street. Maybe I can find some interesting containers for dried-flower arrangements.

When you're finished, meet me there and we can get something to eat."

"I don't even know if Winslow still owns the paper. He could have retired or sold it."

"You won't know until you go in," Maggie said.

"All right," he said, brushing a quick kiss on her forehead. "I'll just be a few minutes."

The office was silent when he walked in. As a bi-weekly, the *Lake Country Register* had always been a small operation with only a few full-time people on staff. Publisher and editor Cal Winslow did nearly every job from selling ad space to laying out the front page. This was journalism at its most basic and Luke couldn't help envying Cal's life, so simple and uncomplicated.

He stepped up to the counter and rang the small bell. "Is anyone here?"

The front door creaked behind him and Luke turned to see a familiar figure stepping inside. "Sorry," Winslow called. "I had to run to the post office." He wiped his feet, then glanced up through foggy glasses. "Now, what can I do for—" He paused and a smile broke across his face. "Luke? Luke Fitzpatrick? Is that you?"

Winslow hadn't aged a day in ten years. He was a slight man with boundless energy and, even now, his step was quick and determined. His once-black hair had turned snow-white, but his features, so keen and perceptive, were unlined.

Luke held out his hand. "Mr. Winslow. It's been a long time."

"Cal," he said, crossing the room to shake Luke's hand. "We're both members of the press corps now. How have you been, Luke? I haven't seen you in..."

"In far too long," Luke said with an apologetic

smile. "Since I graduated from college, at that party my grandmother threw for me."

"Proudest day of my life," Cal said. "My first protégé on his way in the world. How is your grandmother?"

"She lives with her sister now in Phoenix. She's taken up golf."

Cal chuckled and rubbed his chin. "Long time ago. So what brings you back to Potter's Junction?"

Luke shook his head ruefully. "A woman, actually."

"Now, there's an interesting lead." Cal clapped him on the shoulder. "Come on. I've got some coffee back in my office. Let's sit down and you can tell me the rest of the story."

Winslow's office was exactly as Luke had remembered it, a mess of printer's proofs and edited copy overflowing from the scarred oak desk. The smell of newsprint and ink was thick in the air and stacks of the *Register* cluttered nearly every inch of floor space. Luke walked over to the wall and examined the awards and photos that had fascinated him as a kid. He knew all the stories behind each memento, the adventure and the danger that had piqued a young boy's imagination. He could trace his interest in journalism to this very spot.

"Do you ever miss it?" Luke asked, staring up at a photo of Cal dressed in combat fatigues, standing next to a Huey helicopter. Like so many reporters of his generation, he'd covered the war in Vietnam.

"Sometimes," Cal said. "When life gets a little ordinary. When the most exciting story I have to cover is another town meeting or the annual snowmobile festival." He grabbed a photo from his desk and handed it to Luke. "But then I take a good long look at the wife and the kids and the grandkids, and I realize that I've got all I need right here. Besides, a good reporter can find something newsworthy in almost any story, if he looks hard enough."

Luke took a seat in front of Cal's desk. "But you were right in the thick of it. Then you just quit and moved up here to the middle of nowhere. I used to think you were crazy, giving all that up."

"And now?"

Luke rubbed his forehead and frowned. "I don't know. Maybe you had it right all along."

"You sound a little singed. If you go at it too hard, you're bound to burn out," Winslow said, fixing him with a perceptive gaze.

"Is that what happened to you?"

"I'm asking the questions here, Fitzpatrick."

Luke nodded. "Yeah, maybe I am a little fried. I've been working nonstop for the past three years. I used to get so juiced by the excitement. Every assignment was a new challenge, a chance to prove I was the best. But now…now, I'm just tired."

"Tell me about this woman," Cal said, leaning back in his chair and linking his hands behind his head. "Who is she?"

"Remember Maggie Kelley?" Luke asked.

Cal chuckled. "That skinny little girl who used to follow you around town, fetching and carrying and hanging on your every word? That Maggie Kelley?"

Luke nodded. "She's not so skinny anymore. And she certainly doesn't listen to me, at least not lately. We've been friends for years. Then, on New Year's Eve, everything changed. Now I'm not sure what we are."

"So why are you really here, Luke? What do you want me to tell you? Your career is going great, but I'm sure you know that. I have to admit, I get a real kick out of seeing your byline pop up every couple of weeks. You're an ace. There are a thousand and one journalists who would give up their press passes for one day in your shoes."

"But not you," Luke said. He looked over at the wall full of pictures. "When I was a kid I used stare at your photos and dream about what I was going to do, how I wasn't going to stop until I'd won all the awards, until everyone knew Luke Fitzpatrick was the best."

"So you haven't won a Pulitzer yet," Cal said. "You're still young. You've got time."

"But I don't want a Pulitzer anymore. And I don't care about the bylines or the recognition. Right now, I don't even want to get on a plane again."

"That's what you don't want. What *do* you want?"

"I want to get the excitement back, that rush I used to get when a strolled into the middle of a war zone and the day was full of possibilities. The only time I feel that is—" Luke sucked in a sharp breath at the realization. The only time he felt that way lately was when he kissed Maggie.

"Maybe you want the woman more than you want the job," Cal suggested.

Luke shook his head slowly. "No, I don't think so."

Cal shrugged. "Or maybe it is just a little burnout."

"How am I supposed to know?"

"Go back to work," he said. "You'll figure it out soon enough. Either you'll get your chops back or you'll walk away. And if you do walk away, come talk to me. I've got a paper I'm looking to sell."

"I'm supposed to leave this weekend for Albania. I've set up an interview with the leader of the rebel army over there."

"Janaz? Gee, even I envy that assignment."

"You want it? I was supposed to leave on New

Year's Day and I couldn't bring myself to get on the damn plane. Maggie needed me and I wanted to be with her. I don't think there's an editor on this planet who will put up with that kind of behavior for very long."

"Do you want me to tell you what to do?"

Luke nodded. "Yeah. Maybe I do."

Cal pushed forward in his chair and slapped his hands down on the desk. "Well, you've come to the wrong guy, Fitzpatrick. I'm not Dear Abby and I'm not Ann Landers. I'm not your minister or your shrink. You've got to make your own decisions. That's the only way you'll be able to live with them."

Luke let out a tightly held breath. "I guess I already know what I want to do. She's the only constant in my life. And I almost lost her. I'm not going to risk that again."

"So marry her," Cal said.

Luke laughed at the outrageous suggestion. "Marry her?"

"It's done all the time."

"Me? Married?" Luke considered the notion for a long moment. "I guess I could do that. Yeah, I could marry Maggie. But I'm not sure she'd want to marry me. She just wants to be friends."

"Change her mind," Cal said. "Don't give up until she agrees."

Luke stood and reached over Cal's desk to shake his hand. "I should go. I've got to meet Maggie."

Cal clapped him on the shoulder and grabbed his hand. "Hey, we'll trade war stories the next time you're in town. And I'm serious about the paper." He raised his arms and glanced around the office. "All this could be yours."

Luke nodded, then turned and strode through the

front offices. When he reached the sidewalk, he paused for a moment. He had three days before he had to leave for Albania. Right at this moment, all he wanted was Maggie. But would he always feel this way? Or would there come a time when he'd want the old excitement back again, a day when he'd regret choosing her?

As he zipped his jacket, Luke looked up and down the main street of Potter's Junction. Three days. It wasn't much time to make a decision that would change the rest of his life.

"IT LOOKS PRETTIER than I remembered."

Maggie stood on the sidewalk in front of her childhood home and stared at the tiny two-bedroom bungalow. The house looked like a fairy-tale cottage with its freshly painted trim and its quaint front porch. Snow frosted the roof and icicles hung from the gutters. Each detail brought back images of her childhood. Sitting on the front porch with Luke, swinging on the old tire in the backyard, draping colorful Christmas lights around the bushes.

"It's exactly the way I remember it," Luke said, slipping his arm around her shoulders.

"I thought it would hurt to see it, but it doesn't." Maggie sighed. "I guess that's why I stayed away for so long. I hated this place. All the memories. Even though this was my home, I always felt like a guest. Like I was intruding on my mother's life."

"You had a rotten mother," Luke admitted. "But she must have done something right because you turned into a beautiful and kind woman."

She turned and looked up at him, smiling at his sweet compliment. He always knew the right things to say. "I really did love her. Even though I didn't show it. She *was* my mother."

He bent nearer and kissed her softly, his lips brushing against hers. It was a simple gesture, filled with none of the earlier desire. But this kiss was something much more. As Luke gazed down at her, she saw it in his eyes, the unconditional acceptance, the unwavering affection. The assurance that no matter what mistakes they made, he'd always care. Maggie reached up and pressed her palm to his cheek, remembering all the times Luke had been there, with a kind word or gentle encouragement.

"She made it hard," he said, "but you always tried. That's what I admired about you, Maggie. How hard you always tried."

They stood silently, letting the memories wash over them like a warm summer rain. The past mingled with the present, and though she and Luke had come so far from their childhood in Potter's Junction, some things still remained the same. "I can tell you anything," Maggie murmured. "It's always been that way, hasn't it."

Luke chuckled. "You used to tell me *everything*." He pointed to the front steps. "We'd sit right there and you would chatter on and on about all your plans. You always had a plan. Remember those little notebooks you used to carry?"

Maggie frowned, searching her mind for the memory. "No."

"Sure you do. You'd write out endless lists and detailed plans. I remember once you copied the Greyhound bus schedule. You couldn't have been more than eleven or twelve, but you were already planning your escape. Deciding which bus to take and where to go. How much you'd need for bus fare and where you'd have to sit to get the most scenic view."

"I don't remember that."

"And your house. You had a little floor plan all drawn out with lists of all the furniture you'd need to buy. Green polka-dot curtains for the kitchen. Remember?"

A slow smile touched the corners of Maggie's mouth. "Yes," she murmured. "I do remember that." She laughed, a flush of embarrassment warming her cheeks. "Well, it's always good to have a plan."

Maggie linked her arm through his and they started back toward downtown. They stopped at Luke's old house, just down the street, and sneaked into the backyard to see if his initials were still carved into the trunk of an old oak tree. And they did find the faint tracing that he'd made so many years ago, time and weather having worn it away until the scar had nearly healed.

For the rest of the morning, they wandered up and down the streets with no particular destination in mind. They never seemed to run out of things to talk about and Maggie recognized how much she had missed Luke. Just walking beside him, listening to the sound of his voice, enjoying the elaborate way he told a story.

When they reached the downtown area, she realized how hungry she was and pointed to a little coffee shop at the end of the street. As they walked, they paused every now and then to look into a shop window, knowing that, for once, they had all the time in the world. As Luke examined a typewriter in the window of a secondhand shop, Maggie moved along to the next window.

The huge letters painted on the inside of the plate glass stopped her in her tracks. Maggie stared at the sign trumpeting the dire news. GOING OUT OF BUSINESS. INVENTORY REDUCTION SALE. In the corner of the window, a For Sale sign had been posted with the name and number of the local real estate agent.

"Maggie?"

She blinked, then turned to find Luke staring at her. "What?"

"Is everything all right?"

Maggie looked back at the window. "This is a floral shop," she said. "I didn't realize Potter's Junction had a floral shop."

"It doesn't look like they will for too much longer."

She frowned as she peered into the window. "I wonder if it's hard to make a living up here. There have to be weddings and parties. And tourists in the summer. But I suppose the winter could be pretty slow."

"Maybe they just want to move to Florida," Luke suggested.

"If they're going out of business because they want to, then that's all right. But maybe they've made some mistakes, some bad business decisions. A person shouldn't have to give up all they've worked for just because of a few simple mistakes."

Luke grabbed her arms and turned her toward him. "Maggie, what are you talking about?"

Glancing back at the window, she deftly avoided his curious gaze. Why not tell him? All she was really risking was her pride. And Luke always knew what to do, he always gave such good advice. But would he admire her so much once he found out how stupid she'd been? Or would he berate her for letting Colin make her business decisions for her?

In less than two months, she'd be painting a big sign in her front window, alerting everyone who passed to her failure, her naiveté. She'd put her faith in a future that had crumbled before her eyes. And now, she was left to pick up the pieces and paste together a new life.

Maggie took one last look at the floral shop. She could make a success of this place. She wouldn't rely so much on fresh flowers, although that would be part of the business. She'd concentrate on dried florals—swags and garlands and rustic wreaths—creations that tourists would buy in the summer months. In the winter she could give lessons in floral arranging and garden planning. And she'd carry a selection of interesting gift items and maybe a few racks of greeting cards. She could make a success of this place if she had a good plan.

"Maggie?"

She snapped out of her reverie and forced a smile onto her face. "I'm hungry," she said, her mind still caught by the excitement of opening a new shop. It really didn't matter where it was. In truth, she could open a shop anywhere, start with a clean slate and a fresh attitude. Maggie knew that wherever she went next, she'd be a success. There was no longer a need to worry. "Let's try the coffee shop at the end of the street."

She linked her arm through Luke's, her outlook suddenly much brighter. It was a beautiful day, full of possibilities. The sun was shining. Luke was walking beside her. And it was the start of a whole new millennium. Her life might change in unexpected ways, but Maggie was ready for a change.

As they walked to the restaurant, they talked more about the past, about the silly events of their childhood. Maggie was struck by how tangled together their past really was. Memory after memory came rushing back in such detail that she felt as if she were living it all over again. And as she listened to Luke tell another story, she realized that he'd been wrong earlier. It hadn't been her mother who had made Maggie into the person she was today—the strong, determined and capable woman who could take on any challenge and weather any storm. It had been Luke.

It had always been Luke.

THEY HAD DINNER at the little restaurant, the two of them sitting in a quiet booth sipping coffee until they'd both thawed out. They hadn't talked like this since they were kids, Luke mused, and it was obvious Maggie had dearly missed their conversations. Her green eyes were bright and her color high as she chattered on and on about anything that popped into her head.

He'd forgotten how much he loved listening to her voice, watching the way her hands moved when she spoke, the quirky mannerisms he found so endearing. When the waitress stopped at their table to inform them it was closing time, Luke glanced at his watch and saw they'd been talking for nearly four hours. He reluctantly asked for their check.

"I didn't realize how late it was," Maggie said. "I forgot Potter's Junction rolls up the streets at 9:00 p.m." She gathered up her jacket and mittens. "Maybe it's all the caffeine, but I don't feel tired at all."

"Me, neither," Luke replied. The last thing he wanted was to call an end to their time together, to retreat to his own chilly cabin at the While-A-Way to face eight hours of solitude. They'd spent a perfect day together and he couldn't help but want just one perfect night—a night spent in Maggie's bed and in her arms, touching her and making love to her until the morning dawned.

Though Maggie was intent on going backward, back to friendship, Luke could only see what was in front of him. In just a few short days, Maggie had drawn him into her orbit, the pull of her so strong he'd nearly forgotten who he'd been without her. In the past, he had been able to walk away, to leave her behind. Now he felt as if she was leaving him behind, searching for a happiness that might not include him. Hell, she'd nearly married Colin Spencer, a man she didn't love. What was next?

Luke knew he could make Maggie happier than Colin Spencer ever could have. They were kindred souls and they belonged together, maybe not as husband and wife, but together. All he needed was a chance to prove it, a chance to break through the protective wall she'd built around her heart. But Maggie's fears ran deep, all the way back to her childhood.

He tossed a few bills on the table and helped her slip into her jacket. Maybe he should be happy to maintain the status quo, to be satisfied with their friendship. But every instinct told him there was something more here, something he was bound to discover if he just dug a little further.

"It's a beautiful night," she said, staring up at the sky as they walked out of the coffee shop. A slice of the moon hung low over the main street of Potter's Junction and a soft snow had begun to fall, turning the scene into a picture postcard.

Luke slipped his arm around her shoulders and drew her closer. He had spent so little time with Maggie over the past few years he'd forgotten how completely happy she could make him. With just a smile or a sweet word, she turned his world into a pleasant place, a place where he appreciated moonlight and snowflakes, where danger and destruction couldn't touch him.

Maybe that's what this was all about. A man couldn't spend his life trudging through war zones without losing a little piece of his soul. Maggie brought balance to his world. She forced him to remember that he was more than a reporter and she always showed him the joy of simple things. And when he had been renewed, Luke went right back to the battlefront. But this time was different.

He hadn't thought about work since he'd left Chicago and he had no urge to go back. This was exactly where he wanted to be, with Maggie, talking to her, holding her close, spending the day gazing into her pretty face. Luke suspected, sooner or later, he'd feel restless again and he'd be compelled to leave. But something was keeping him here now and he wasn't about to fight it.

"I had a nice time today," he said as they strolled down the sidewalk.

A winsome smile touched her lips. "Me, too. We always have a good time when we're together."

They walked past the post office and the VFW hall, past the school and the Lutheran church. They simply wandered, neither one of them willing to call an end to the night. But the cold wind soon forced them back to the While-A-Way, to the front steps of Maggie's cabin. And to another bout with temptation.

He didn't want to retire to his cabin and didn't want her to disappear inside hers. When she reached for her key in her pocket, Luke took his chance and grabbed her around the waist, picking her up off her feet. Together, they tumbled in a snowbank, Maggie yelping in surprise.

"What are you doing?" she cried, tossing a handful of snow in his face.

"I don't want to go in just yet." Luke leaned over her, bracing his hand near her head. He grinned and blinked the snow off his own lashes, then leaned closer. With exquisite care, he kissed her cheek, the icy crystals on it melting beneath his warm lips. Slowly, he moved across to her nose, then to her forehead, placing one lingering kiss at each stop.

She didn't breathe and, for a long moment, he thought she might pull away. But then her arms came around his neck and she drew him closer. Luke groaned softly, rolling her over on top of him and taking her wet face between his palms.

Slowly, tentatively, their mouths met and this time, for the first time, there was no doubt. They both wanted this, this tantalizing meeting of lips and tongues, warm breath mingling and clouding around them. With every second that passed, the kiss grew more perfect and more intense. Everything they felt for each other became focused on this connection.

Maggie grabbed his jacket and pulled him on top of her, urgent sounds slipping from her throat. She stretched out, her body so soft and warm beneath his. Nothing had prepared him for the wild sensations that pulsed through his bloodstream. He'd never wanted a woman so badly, never needed a woman to want him. Any vestige of self-control was gone and he needed to make love to Maggie here and now.

As they rolled around like children in the snow, passion mixed with playfulness. Luke knew their relationship had shifted, taken a sudden, new direction. He'd felt only resistance and doubt from Maggie before this. With one mind-numbing kiss, her reluctance had dissolved. She had responded to him, arching toward him, searching for more, impatient and insistent.

But now that they'd reached this turning point, he understood her earlier apprehension. The next step would transform them from friends to lovers. And with that transformation came expectations. Could he be the man Maggie needed? Or would that require completely altering his life?

That prospect didn't seem so disagreeable when he put it alongside a life with Maggie Kelley. His professional accomplishments had never really mattered to her. Maggie's loyalties to him were unconditional and unwavering. Hell, he could dig ditches and she'd still make him feel like a success.

When he finally drew back and looked into Maggie's eyes, she smiled. "Maybe we should go inside. I'm cold," she said.

Without a second thought, he drew her to her feet and into his embrace, rubbing her back with his palms. They stood there for a long time, touching as they brushed snow from each other's clothing. "I want to kiss you again," he murmured, his lips finding the warm pulse point on her neck.

"I—I want you to kiss me," Maggie said. "Long and hard and for the rest of the night. But I'm afraid."

He drew back and stared into her wide eyes, surprised. "What are you afraid of?"

Maggie shrugged, then looked away. "I'm just afraid we might make a mistake. That we'll regret this someday and we'll want to take it all back."

Luke stroked her cheek in an attempt to soothe her doubts and regain his composure. "Then maybe we should wait. I don't ever want to hurt you, Maggie. And I promise, I won't. But you have to be sure."

A war between passion and practicality played out in her eyes. In the end, she pushed up on her toes and gave him a quick hug. "Maybe we should sleep on it tonight. Things will be clearer in the morning."

Reluctantly, Luke nodded his assent. He watched her open her door and disappear inside the room. Leaning back against the wall beside the door, Luke furrowed his hands through his hair and cursed softly. He reached out and touched the door, drawing his palm down to the knob, tempted to test it.

Instinct told him Maggie would always have doubts, that they would come to this point again and again, then turn back. Drawing a deep breath, he moved away from the door and walked toward his room. Maybe he wanted too much. In his experience, life usually took the logical course. And logic told him that friends weren't meant to be lovers.

8

His LIPS BURNED a path across her body, from her neck to her shoulder, and then, to her breast. She arched against him as he lingered there, his mouth teasing the hard nipple, his tongue stoking her passion until she felt as if she might be engulfed in desire.

"Luke," she pleaded. "Oh, Luke."

He answered her with actions, not with words. She closed her eyes and let the sensation of his mouth on her body fuel her need. Every nerve tingled, her blood blazing through her veins like wildfire through tinder. She wanted to touch him but when she reached for him, he eluded her. He was there. She could feel him, but she couldn't see him. His mouth drifted lower, to her belly and then lower still.

Her hips pressed up, urging him to go farther. When he touched her there, at the center of her need, a powerful tremor shook her body. All her breath left her lungs in a single, ragged cry of release.

"Luke!"

Maggie's eyes flew open and she blinked, once and then twice. Slowly, she pushed aside the haze of sleep that muddled her mind. For a long moment, she wasn't sure where she was. As her eyes focused in the gray light of dawn, she picked out the details of her surroundings. She recognized the interior of her cabin at the While-A-Way Lodge, the flowered drapes and the knotty-pine paneling.

Pressing her palm to her chest, she felt her heart thudding beneath her fingers like a tin drum. A thin sheen of perspiration cooled her hot skin and she kicked at the blankets, then struggled to sit up, her breath still coming in quick gasps.

"What is wrong with me?" she murmured, raking her fingers through her damp, tangled hair. Though she didn't often remember her dreams, she certainly recalled every vivid detail about this one! She'd been in the midst of a passionate encounter with Luke Fitzpatrick, an encounter that was already replaying itself over and over in her head. His hands and his mouth, his warm breath teasing her skin. It had all been so incredibly…real.

Maggie sucked in a sharp breath, then pressed her fingertips to her temples, trying to drive the images from her brain. It wasn't as if she'd never thought about him in that way. Lately, she'd been almost obsessed. But in all her fantasies, she'd never been so aware of the power he could wield. She'd never imagined that he could possess her mind and her body, her very soul, the way he had in her dream. There had been no anxiety, no inhibition, in her behavior. She'd given herself over to him completely.

"I can't do this to myself," she said, clutching the sheet in her fists.

She could try to put him out of her mind during the day. It was easy enough to occupy her thoughts with less intriguing matters—the scenery, the weather, the price of beaded moccasins. But how could she stop her dreams? Now that he'd come to her once, she knew he'd be back, night after night, until she turned her fantasy into reality.

Maggie crawled out of bed and began to pace the room, desperate for a solution to her delicate problem.

After careful thought, only one option to her dilemma came to mind. She'd simply have to make love with Luke Fitzpatrick.

She stopped pacing and considered the notion for no more than an instant before tossing it aside. Was she out of her mind? Making love with Luke would be the worst thing she could possibly do! Once she'd experienced him in the most intimate way, there would be no going back. The fact that she couldn't stop kissing him should have taught her that much. She plopped down on the edge of the bed, then quickly stood up again.

It wouldn't be that difficult. She could simply put on her shoes, walk to his cabin and knock on his front door. If everything went the way it had in her dream, she wouldn't even have to speak. He'd know exactly what she was there for, wouldn't he? And even if he didn't, she'd just throw herself into his arms and kiss him until his manly instincts took over. Maggie groaned as a warm blush crept up her cheeks. She couldn't even think about the prospect without embarrassment. She'd never seduced a man in her life.

"All right," she said, sitting down on the end of the bed. "There have to be other choices." At the moment, nothing came immediately to mind. Every thought in her head was focused on walking out of the cabin right into Luke's bed and reliving the dream she'd just had.

"I have to get away. I have to put some distance between us." But how would she manage that? They'd spent nearly every waking hour together since he'd arrived in Potter's Junction. Avoiding his company was impossible. And even if she tried, he wouldn't make it easy.

"I could go back to Chicago," she said, testing the alternative against her earlier plan.

It only took a heartbeat to realize that this was her

only choice. Maggie stood up and began to gather her clothes. She threw her suitcase on the bed and dumped her things inside, not bothering to fold or arrange as she always did. In between fits of packing, she got dressed, tugging on whatever was handy.

When she finished, she took a last look around the cabin, then hurried to the door. But she stopped there, realizing what she was about to do. She couldn't just walk out on him. He'd wake up and he wouldn't know where she'd gone. Knowing Luke, he'd probably assume the worst—that she'd been kidnapped by drunken snowmobilers or abducted by deranged ice fishermen.

"A note," she murmured, dropping her bags in front of the door. "I'll leave him a note."

Maggie found a stack of While-A-Way stationery in the top drawer of the desk. She grabbed a pen from her purse and sat down, carefully composing her missive in her head. "Dear Luke," she murmured, scribbling the words on the paper.

It was a start, but the rest would need to be more carefully worded. She'd need an excuse, a reason beyond reproach. "Sorry to leave but there's an emergency at the store." Maggie smiled. An emergency was good. If he asked, she could tell him the security system had gone haywire or one of her coolers had shorted out. And she'd get Kim to back her up. Heck, maybe by the time she got back to Chicago, there would be a real emergency to replace the lie she'd told.

Maggie bent over the paper and wrote a few last words. "Call me when you get back. Love, Maggie."

She stared at her closing, a frown wrinkling her forehead. "*Love.* That's too strong a word." She crossed it out. "Fondly, Maggie. Or maybe, Sincerely, Maggie." She pulled another sheet of While-A-Way stationery from the desk drawer and recopied the note. "Just Maggie," she said as she signed her name with a flourish.

She carefully folded the note, then took one final look around the cabin before tossing the key onto a table beside the door. She wouldn't bother waking the manager since he already had her credit-card number. As she stepped outside into the crisp winter air, the sun peeked above the eastern horizon. The sky was clear, the last stars of the night quickly fading.

Taking care not to make noise, Maggie dragged her luggage to the van and tossed it inside. She scraped the frost off the windows and started the engine, letting it warm while she walked over to Luke's cabin. The snow crunched beneath her feet and she listened for a moment at the door, but didn't hear a sound. Holding her breath, she bent down and slipped the note beneath the door, then turned and ran to her van.

A few seconds later she was out of the parking lot and onto the main highway that led south to Chicago. The first mile seemed to fly by, but as her mind began to clear, she couldn't help wondering about what she'd just done. She'd run away again. The only difference this time was that she'd bothered to formulate an excuse beforehand.

Sure, he'd be angry. Or maybe he'd be hurt. He'd certainly be confused. But she'd have to deal with that later. Right now, she didn't trust herself within one hundred yards of Luke Fitzpatrick. The man had an uncanny knack for testing the limits of their friendship, a friendship she was determined to preserve.

MAGGIE SAT in the center of her bed and shivered, her body trembling from head to toe, her teeth chattering. She'd tried to sleep, but once again dreams of Luke had plagued her mind. Adding to her troubles, the heat had gone off in the coach house a few hours ago. She'd made a late-night call to her landlord and then tried a long list of twenty-four-hour heating contractors. But the repairmen in Chicago had been swamped with calls since the first of the year. All the power outages and power surges caused by the millennium bug had caused furnaces all over town to stop in protest.

With a low groan, she crawled out of bed and wrapped her chenille robe more tightly around her. She was already dressed in two layers and had added a few more blankets to the bed, but it didn't do much to ward off the falling temperature in the house. The icy wind seemed to blow into every crack and crevice.

The thermostat read sixty degrees, but as another shiver raced through her limbs, she realized it wasn't the cold that was affecting her so deeply. It was her indecision, all the nagging doubts that had plagued her mind since she'd left Potter's Junction.

She was in love with Luke Fitzpatrick! She had probably loved him for years and never allowed herself to admit it. But now her fantasies had finally intruded on reality. Of course she loved him! Once again, he'd played the white knight at a time when she'd been completely vulnerable. And worse, she'd allowed herself to be carried away with the illusion that they might ride off into the sunset and find a happily-ever-after together.

She now knew that's why she hadn't been able to give her heart to Colin, why she had felt only relief at their broken engagement. She'd secretly loved Luke Fitzpatrick. Maggie drew her knees up and rested her chin on them, tugging the blankets more tightly around her.

"It's not my fault," she murmured. "It's in my

genes." Her mother had perfected the art of loving the wrong man and now Maggie was following in her footsteps. Luke could never love her. He was obsessed with his work.

Over the years, Maggie had learned to recognize the signs. He would come home, worn-out, exhausted from whatever assignment he'd just completed. They would see each other and talk, share a few laughs, stroll down memory lane. And slowly, he'd begin to gain back his energy. Then one day, she'd see the restlessness, the way his eyes looked past her, as if he were already on a plane to some distant war zone. The next thing she knew, he'd be gone.

Maggie sighed. She wasn't going to make the same mistakes her mother had made. If she worked hard enough and set her mind to it, Maggie could fall out of love as easily as she had fallen into it. She would stop thinking about his kisses…and his incredible body… and the haze of desire that hooded his blue eyes when he touched her. She could put all that aside with the proper dose of determination.

Still, there was one thing standing in the way of complete success—overwhelming curiosity. Maybe that's why she'd been drawn to him this time around. It was only natural to speculate about what it might be like between them. And as long as that curiosity crackled with every touch, Maggie knew she'd never be able to think of him as just a friend.

That was why she'd kissed him that night on her front porch—she'd admitted as much to Luke. And that was why she continued to question the bounds of their friendship. If she made love with Luke Fitzpatrick, she could put her infatuation into proper perspective. She could stop looking at him as a hero and start to see him as a man—a man who she could never love. A man who could never love her.

"You should have slept with him," she murmured. "If you had satisfied your curiosity, you wouldn't have to fantasize about him for the rest of your life."

She flopped back on the bed, dragging the covers over her head. Would making love with Luke put an end to this infatuation? She'd been curious about kissing him, but the more he kissed her the more she seemed to enjoy it. Maybe making love with him would be equally addictive.

Maggie rolled over and pulled the pillow around her cold ears, another storm of doubt raining down on her. But a sound intruded on her thoughts, a ringing and a banging that wouldn't go away. She sat up in bed and tossed the pillow aside. A loud knock sounded on the front door, followed by the doorbell.

Her breath froze in her throat and she clutched her hands to her chest, then scrambled out of bed. When she reached the front door, she hesitated, her hand on the knob. She knew who was standing on the other side and every instinct told her to run back to bed and hide under the covers. But an inexplicable force made her unlock the dead bolt. With a trembling hand, she reached out and opened the door.

Luke stood beneath the harsh light on her front stoop. His clothes were rumpled and the rough stubble of a beard darkened his cheeks. He shifted uneasily, then looked directly into her eyes. "I got your note," he said.

"I—I had to get home. There was an...emergency."

"You know, Maggie, I really thought we were friends."

"We—we are."

"A friend wouldn't just run out like that in the middle of the night."

"It wasn't the middle of the night," she said. "It was really early in the morning. And a real friend would understand."

He smiled ruefully and shook his head. "I guess you're right. A friend would understand." With a soft curse, he spun away and started down the front steps. But then he stopped short. For a long time, he stood with his back to her. Then slowly, he turned back. "I don't want to be your friend anymore."

Maggie's breath caught in her throat. "Wha-what?"

He climbed the front steps until he stood in front of her. "You heard me. I don't think we should be friends."

"But—but—I don't understand."

In one smooth movement, he grabbed her around the waist and yanked her body against his, pushing them both into the house. He kicked the door closed, then swung her around until her back was pressed against the door. Maggie cried out in surprise as his mouth came down on hers, desperate and demanding. He drew back and stared into her eyes, his gaze fierce. "It's not enough anymore, Maggie. Not nearly enough."

Her knees went weak as he kissed her again. But Maggie knew Luke wouldn't let her fall. He held tight to her as if he might never let her go. Every doubt that she had vanished in a single instant, that moment when she tossed aside her resistance and surrendered to him. He'd been her friend for most of her life and now he was about to become her lover. There was no one in the world she could trust with her heart, except Luke. And nothing she had experienced before had prepared her for the power of her desire for him.

"What are we doing?" she murmured as he ravaged her mouth.

With a soft curse, Luke shoved his fingers through her hair and tugged her head back, forcing her gaze up to his. She saw raw need in his eyes, so intense it sent a shiver along her spine. "We're putting an end to our friendship," he said, ripping off his leather jacket and tossing it aside. "Here and now."

His mouth pressed against the base of her throat and Maggie let out a strangled moan. "I don't want to be friends. Not tonight."

With that, he reached down, scooped her into his arms and carried her to the bedroom. He gently set her down beside the bed. The room had become frigid, but oddly Maggie didn't feel the cold. Her pulse thrummed in her head and her blood raced through her body, warming her limbs until every nerve tingled with anticipation.

"Tell me what you want," he murmured, his lips tracing a line along her collarbone as he pushed aside her robe. The heavy chenille slipped along her bare arms and dropped around her feet.

"I—I want you," Maggie said. "With me...in my bed."

Luke nuzzled aside her T-shirt and gently bit her shoulder. "What else. Tell me. I want to know."

Maggie wasn't sure what to say. Her needs had never been a part of her sexual experiences, nor had a lengthy discussion of those needs. But with Luke, she felt like a different woman, provocative, uninhibited. She could say anything to him and it would be all right. "I want you to take off your shirt," she finally said.

A lazy grin curled his lips and he stepped back. He slowly unbuttoned the shirt, then shrugged it off his shoulders and let it slip down his arms. When it reached his wrists, he let go of the cuffs and the shirt fell to the floor. Maggie let her eyes skim over his torso, from the sharp angles of his shoulders to the sleek muscles of his belly. She reached out and traced her finger along the line of dark hair that ran from his collarbone to the top button of his jeans.

He reached for the waistband, but Maggie drew a quick breath and stopped his hand. "No," she murmured.

"If you don't want to, we—"

"No," Maggie interrupted. "I want to. I'm just a little nervous. My—my knees are shaking."

Luke grasped her waist and picked her up off her feet, pressing his lips into the soft valley between her breasts. Slowly, he let her slide down along his body, their clothes causing a delicious friction between them, until their hips met, until she could feel his desire though the soft fabric of his jeans. Gently, he lowered her onto the bed and stretched out over her, taking all his weight on his arms.

Maggie had never experienced the mind-numbing passion that was supposed to accompany lovemaking. But then, she'd never truly made love. And though she didn't want to love Luke, she had to. Just for this one night. She stared up into his eyes and smiled. "Nothing has ever felt this right," she said.

He bent lower and brushed her lips with his. "Oh, Maggie, I need you." With a low growl, Luke let his arms collapse and his full weight sank against her body. Maggie ran her hands over his shoulders. Hard muscle and smooth skin warmed beneath her palms and she marveled at how glorious it was to touch him without restraint.

His mouth tormented her, exploring every inch of skin with languid passion. Strange new sensations shot through her body with every touch and, suddenly, Maggie desperately needed to feel nothing between them but heat and skin.

With impatient hands, they tugged and tore and twisted at each other's clothes. His jeans slid down his long muscular legs and he kicked them off. Maggie's breath stilled in her chest as she took in the raw beauty of his naked body, the subtle power of his arousal.

She wriggled out of her sweatpants, the cold air of the coach house immediately cooling her hot skin. His fingers slid beneath the T-shirt she wore and he pushed it up, bunching the fabric in his fists along the way. She raised her arms over her head and she watched as Luke's gaze raked along the full length of her body. Nothing stood between them now, not the past or the future. They would have this one night together and that would be all.

The world had fallen away and Maggie knew this was destiny at work. He'd touched her years ago with such sweet innocence, two children with only friendship between them. Maybe they were meant to reach this point, to know one exquisite night of passion between them. Maybe it would make their friendship that much deeper. Maggie was willing to take the chance.

Luke placed his fingertips at the base of her neck and slowly traced a line to her breasts, to her belly and then lower. He could have taken her then and there, but instead he touched her with compelling tenderness, waiting and watching until the time was right.

She had never felt easy with her body, always unsure of what she had to offer a man. But as she looked at Luke, she saw herself through his eyes. To him, she was sexy and beautiful and perfect, and his hands told her just that with every caress.

Maggie arched against his palm and his fingers drifted lower, searching, teasing until he found her moist core. She cried out as electric pulses surged through her. His name slipped from her lips again and again, a soft plea for release. But every time she came close to the edge, he drew her back.

The knot of tension tightened, threatening to snap. And then, in one smooth and sure motion, Luke grabbed her waist and pulled her on top of him. Her knees straddled his hips and she felt his arousal between her legs, hard and hot. She tipped her head back and gave herself over to the sweet sensations of his hands, his erection tantalizing her with even the slightest movement.

Why hadn't she known? All these years and she'd never realized how it could be between them. She'd been afraid to go this far but now that they were together, she feared nothing. Maggie felt alive, on fire, swept up in the moment. She'd become a different person in Luke's arms.

"When are you going to take this off?" he murmured, toying at the ring she still wore on her left hand.

She stared at her hand for a long moment. "I—I've tried. I couldn't get it off."

His gaze fixed on her, his blue eyes intense with purpose. He took hold of her finger and put it into his mouth, sucking gently, sensually, until her entire hand tingled with strange sensations. Then he held her hand out in front of him and slowly twisted the ring, easily moving it over her knuckle. Suddenly, she was free, just like that, as if Colin had never existed. Luke reached over and tossed the ring on the bedside table, then turned back to her.

"He's out of your life," he murmured, his thumbs

brushing the hard nubs of her nipples. "And we're together now."

Maggie drew a sharp breath as a frisson of electricity shot through her body. Tipping her head back, she reveled in the exquisite pleasure of his hands and then his mouth on her breasts. She felt light-headed, as if she was losing touch with reality. But then, this wasn't reality at all. With every minute that passed, they sank further into a world of their own, where touch took the place of words, where the past didn't matter.

And when she finally sheathed him and he slipped inside her, Maggie held her breath, certain she would wake from this strange and powerful dream. She had never wanted to love Luke, but she did. Her soul had been his from the very beginning and now he possessed her body as well, a body that cried out for release.

Slowly, patiently, he began to move. Soft words became urgent pleas and passion surged between them. And when he closed his eyes and tensed beneath her, Maggie let go. With one deep and sure stroke, he was there. And in a shattering instant, she joined him, aching and breathless.

Why had it taken so long for them to find each other? Why had she fought so hard to keep from loving him? Here, wrapped in his arms, Maggie knew with absolute certainty this man was her life. And nothing she could do would keep her from loving him.

THIS TIME, when Luke woke up, Maggie was still asleep next to him. He sighed and turned his face into her pale hair, pulling her body against his until her backside was tucked snugly into his lap. He could spend weeks just like this, lying in bed with her curled against him.

Luke knew they'd have to get back to their everyday

lives sooner or later, but right now, he didn't want to leave Maggie's bed. The rest of the world seemed so unimportant when compared to what he'd experienced with Maggie. This was the last place he had expected to spend the first week of the new millennium. Had events transpired differently, he could have been sitting in a rain-soaked tent in Albania, trying to keep his feet from freezing and his computer from shorting out.

His thoughts drifted back to the night before and a fresh flood of desire warmed his blood. Never in a thousand years would he have imagined this, Maggie, naked in his arms, the warm flush of their lovemaking still fresh in his mind. Luke gently brushed the hair from her nape and pressed his lips against the curve of her neck.

Maggie moaned softly in her sleep. Luke kissed her again and again, trailing his lips across her shoulders and down to the small of her back. Finally, she drew a deep breath and rolled over, giving him a sleepy smile.

He'd never looked at Maggie as anything more than a sweet and naive woman. But after last night, he realized he'd been completely oblivious to the passion simmering just below the surface. He'd never shared such an intense experience with a woman, so perfect and complete.

"Why are you trying so hard to wake me up?" she murmured, rubbing the sleep from her eyes.

"I was lonely," Luke said, dropping a quick kiss between her breasts.

Maggie sighed softly as his lips traced a lazy path down her belly. The smell of their lovemaking filled his head, causing him to grow hard with need. He teased at her silken skin with his teeth and tongue, soft gasps of pleasure slipping from her lips and disappearing in the cold air of her bedroom.

He'd never needed a woman the way he needed Maggie. Everything about her—the taste of her mouth, the feel of her fingers in his hair, the wonderful sensation of her naked body pressed against his—every moment he spent in her arms bought him closer to pure paradise.

He remembered the instant he had slipped inside of her for the first time. Luke had never experienced such an intense reaction, overwhelming power mixed with a disturbing vulnerability. His self-control had vanished in a single heartbeat and he found himself lost in the exquisite act of joining his body with hers.

This was what it must be to make love, for what they shared had more to do with an emotional connection than just a physical release. With every stroke, he'd reveled in the fact that it was Maggie beneath him, above him and around him. Sweet Maggie who had taken him to heights of passion he never knew existed. Lovely Maggie whose body had tempted him again and again throughout the night, as if he couldn't possibly get enough of her.

Luke glanced up to gaze into her beautiful face, bracing his hands beside her hips. Her eyes were closed and her head tipped back. With a soft chuckle, he moved lower, inch by tantalizing inch. He paused for a long moment, wanting her to submit to her desire, waiting for a sign that she needed him as much as he wanted her.

"Tell me what you want," he murmured, pressing his lips against the inside of her thigh.

"I want you to kiss me," she said, her breath ragged, her demand catching in her throat.

He drew his tongue up along her other thigh and Maggie arched against him. "Here?" he asked.

"Higher," she said, her lips curling into a playful smile.

He bit the skin beneath her hipbone. "Here?"

With a frustrated moan, Maggie ran her fingers through his hair and tugged his head up. "Don't tease me," she warned, a mischievous glint in her eye. "I'm not about to draw you a map."

He bent lower, his hair brushing her thighs. Gently, he parted her legs and found the spot he'd been searching for, the true center of her passion. She didn't hesitate to moan with pleasure when his tongue found the moist nub. Like she had done the night before, she gave herself over to him completely, pushing aside any inhibitions she may have still harbored, easy with her own body and the powerful reactions his touch caused.

This was the Maggie he wanted, the Maggie he'd never known existed until last night. She belonged to him, completely and irrevocably. And he knew deep in his soul that no man had ever made her feel this way, no man had shared such brazen intimacies with her.

Slowly, he brought her to the edge with his mouth, his movements first slow and gentle, then quickening with the sound of her shallow breathing. She was so close and he wanted her to fall, to release that final bit of control to him. But Maggie wasn't willing to settle for her own pleasure and when she'd reached the limits of her endurance, she softly called his name, her fingers brushing the hair from his eyes.

At that moment, Luke couldn't refuse her anything, no matter how much he wanted to experience bringing her to her peak in this way. With a low growl, he moved up along her body, settling his hips between hers. And when their gazes locked, he kissed her, long and deep, the sweet taste of her sex still lingering in his mouth.

She took her time with the condom, stroking and caressing him with her fingers and her lips until she was satisfied that he had joined her near the edge. And when he finally slipped inside of her, he could barely stand to move. They both froze, their breathing stilled to just a whisper, their bodies tense with need.

Then, when he could stand it no longer, Luke moved just once. He called out her name and she answered with a soft plea of "Now." Together, they both came to a shattering climax, their bodies pulsing and rocking to ultimate completion.

It was a long time before Luke floated back to reality, until his pulse calmed to a normal rate and his breath grew slow and even. He pressed his face into the curve of her neck, nibbling gently on the ridge of her collarbone. "I don't ever want to leave your bed," he said. "But I'm not sure how much more of this I can take."

Maggie scraped her nails along his spine. "I suppose it would be a little decadent to spend the entire day in the pursuit of pleasure."

"We could go get some breakfast," Luke suggested. "Maybe we could go skating downtown. I think I need to do something a little less strenuous."

Maggie smiled and nuzzled his chest. "I kind of enjoy lying here. And it's a lot warmer than ice skating."

"Warm? This place is freezing," he said, shuddering dramatically.

"The furnace is acting up. I think the power surges earlier this week fried the thermostat. No matter how high I turn it, the temperature doesn't get above sixty degrees."

Luke chuckled and kissed the top of her head. "Not to worry. I suppose I could try to keep you warm."

"This could be considered an official winter activity, you know. That's why so many kids are born nine months after a cold snap. It's a good way to keep from freezing." She glanced up at him and the smile faded from her face. "Not that we'll be having any…"

"No," Luke replied. "At least, not any time soon." But the notion tugged at his thoughts. Maggie was a part of his life now and with that came the realization he'd have to make a few changes. They'd have to get married, for one thing. And they'd need to find a place to live, a place big enough for the two of them. And he'd have to figure out how to make his job work with a wife in his life. And then, there were kids. And an even bigger place to live. Maggie would want kids and he—

"Luke?"

He blinked. "What?"

"You seemed a million miles away."

"Not a million," he said. "Maybe a few hundred."

"You were thinking about work, weren't you?"

Luke shook his head. "No. I swear, I wasn't thinking about work. In fact, I haven't thought about work in…days."

"You'll have to go back soon," she said. "When do you have to leave?"

Luke wrapped his arms around her and pulled her against his body, his fingers weaving through her silken hair. "I'm not leaving. I'm staying right here."

"Unfortunately, I don't get a lot of rebel uprisings and botched assassinations here in my bedroom." Maggie sighed. "I don't want to leave this place, either. But we're going to have to go out sooner or later." She rolled over and reached out to pick up the diamond ring on the bedside table, then stared at it for a long moment. "And I'm going to have to talk to Colin."

The mention of Spencer's name brought a sharp stab of anger. "Mail it back to him," he said. "You don't have to talk to that jerk."

She looked at him, then shook her head. "No, I need to talk to him. I need to find out why."

Luke shook his head. "And what good will that do? What will that change?"

"At least I'd know," Maggie said.

"Know what?"

"If—if it was my fault. If I did something wrong."

Luke pushed back and looked down into her eyes. "Your fault? You think what happened was *your* fault?"

"Well, maybe it *is* genetic," Maggie said, averting her eyes. "I mean, my mother had a hard time hanging on to men. Maybe, I—"

"Maggie, stop. You're not your mother. Not even close." He took her face between his hands and forced her to look into his eyes. "We can't control who we love or who we want. It just happens. We feel it deep inside and nothing we do will make it go away. Your mother loved being in love. She became addicted to that rush of longing that makes your heart beat faster and your mind spin in circles. And when that faded, she looked for someone else to give it to her."

"I can control who I love," Maggie said.

"No, you can't," he said, squeezing her arms. "None of us can."

Conflicting emotions filled her eyes and Luke knew she heard the truth in his words. But Maggie Kelley had stubbornly learned to protect her heart, at all costs, and he could sense her rebuilding the wall they'd demolished just moments before. He cursed his honesty. Why did he always have to push her?

"You—you don't love me," she said.

"And what if I do?"

"But we're friends."

"Friends don't share what we've just shared."

"You *can't* love me," Maggie said.

"Why?" he challenged. "Are you going to tell me you don't love me? Because, if you do, I won't believe you."

"I—I'm not sure how I feel," she said, stunned by his admission. "This has all happened so fast. We haven't really thought it through."

"What's to think about?"

"Your work, for one. And my work. The past and the future. Up until a week ago, I was ready to marry Colin Spencer."

"Forget Colin," Luke said.

"I can't just forget him. Technically, I'm still engaged to him."

"You took off the ring last night, Maggie. As far as I'm concerned, he's out of your life for good."

"It's more complicated than that. I was with him for two years. I can't act as if he never existed. Sooner or later, I'm going to have to face him. We're going to have to talk."

"What is this hold he has over you, Maggie? He walked out on you, on the very night you were supposed to announce your engagement—with Isabelle, a woman who was supposed to be your friend."

"I don't need a recap of that night," she said. "I remember it all quite vividly."

"And then, he has the nerve to call me up and ask me to—"

"What did you say?"

Luke winced inwardly. The words had just slipped out, propelled by his growing frustration. But he couldn't take them back. He closed his eyes, wondering if there was any way to correct his mistake, whether there was any explanation she'd accept. He should have told her he'd talked to Colin. But like she said, everything had happened so fast. And he never seemed to find the right spot to slip it into the conversation.

Well, it had been slipped in now, and he'd have to deal with it. But this time, he wasn't going to let Colin Spencer come between him and Maggie again. As far as he was concerned, the only man in Maggie's life, now and forever, would be Luke Fitzpatrick.

9

MAGGIE PUSHED up on her elbow and stared down into Luke's eyes, stunned nearly speechless by his admission. Could she have misunderstood? "You—you talked to Colin?"

Luke nodded, raking his fingers through his hair. "Yeah, I did."

"When?"

He seemed reluctant to answer, but Maggie wasn't about to back down. If Luke knew why Colin had walked out, didn't she deserve an explanation? The man was her fiancé—or he had been until last night. "When?" she repeated.

"He called me on New Year's Day." Luke shook his head. "The guy has a lot of nerve. First, he walks out on you, then he asks me to keep an eye on you until he gets back. He claimed he had some problems to take care of, but he—" Luke took a long breath. "He's still planning to marry you."

Maggie's breath slowly left her body, replaced by an uneasy sense of disbelief. She had barely thought of Colin over the past couple of days. After making love to Luke, her engagement seemed like it had happened to a different person in a different lifetime. But Luke's revelation brought it all back, the confusion, the humiliation. And there was something else that nagged at her mind. She and Luke had always been honest with each other. Why had he kept something so important from her? "He called and you didn't tell me?"

Luke slowly pushed up, concern etching his handsome features. "I guess I didn't think it was important. It's *not* important, is it? Not anymore. You don't love him. You told me you didn't."

She couldn't stop the slow simmer of indignation bubbling deep inside her. How could she have been such a fool? She'd trusted Luke, only to learn he never trusted her! He didn't believe she could run her own life, or draw her own conclusions about Colin and her future. "Don't you think that was my decision to make?" she asked, trying to keep her voice calm and even. "Colin Spencer was my fiancé, not yours," she said, looking away.

He took her chin between his fingers and turned her gaze to his. "Are you angry with me?"

Cursing softly, Maggie grabbed the sheet and tucked it around her breasts. "Yes. Maybe I am. I can make my own decisions, you know. I'm not some half-wit with feathers for brains."

He laughed, then nuzzled her neck. "I realize that."

She stiffened beside him. "Then why didn't you tell me you'd talked to him?"

"Maggie, I just didn't think about it. I meant to tell you that day at the ice rink, but you seemed so… happy. I didn't want to hurt you."

"My fiancé runs off with my girlfriend, he calls and you just forget? Is that your excuse? Because if it is, it's pretty lame." Maggie could see his frustration rising, but she didn't care. She was spoiling for a fight, she wanted him angry. She wanted to push him away, to prove she didn't love him at all.

"I'm not making any excuses," he said. "I just didn't

think it was important. He was gone, out of your life. Good riddance."

Maggie stood up and yanked the tangled sheet along with her, leaving him completely naked on the bed. A current of desire shot through her as her gaze took in his perfect body, the impossibly wide shoulders and narrow waist. She closed her eyes and turned away, before her attention dropped lower, to more intimate territory. "I'm tired of you treating me like I can't make my own decisions. You don't have to protect me!"

The bed creaked as he pushed off it. "Damn it, Maggie, I *want* to protect you. You're the most important thing in the world to me. Why shouldn't I do everything I can to make your life as safe and happy as possible?"

"Because it's *my* life!" she said, pressing her palm to her chest. "Mine! And if I want to marry Colin Spencer, then it's none of your business."

"You don't want to marry Spencer," he said, his jaw tight.

"How do you know?" Maggie countered. "Maybe I will if he still wants me. The point is, I can. And you can't do anything about it."

He grabbed her arm and yanked her against his naked body. Heat snaked through her veins and her knees went weak. He bent close until his lips were nearly touching hers. For a moment, she thought he might kiss her. If he kissed her, it would be all over. Once his lips touched hers, Maggie knew she would forgive him anything.

"Don't play games with me, Maggie. This is too important. You're not going to marry Colin Spencer. I'm not going to let you. You took that ring off last night. You're not engaged anymore."

Maggie pulled out of his grasp, turned and began to

gather his clothes from the floor of her bedroom. "He doesn't know that."

"You're not going to marry him," Luke repeated, his voice cold and even.

She threw the pile of clothes at him, and he caught them, covering at least part of his naked body. "There once was a time when I would have listened to you. I would have done whatever you told me. I trusted you, the same way I trusted Colin."

"And you can still trust me."

"No. The only person I can trust is myself." She tightened the sheet around her body and waited impatiently for him to get dressed. "I want you to leave."

"Why?" he asked, crossing his arms over his bare chest. "I have no intention of walking away from this. Not until you admit that you don't want Spencer."

"All right. Where are my clothes?" Maggie dropped to her knees, clutching at the sheet as she looked under the bed. She found her shoes there and pulled them out, then retrieved her jeans and sweater from the floor and struggled to her feet.

"Where are you going?"

"I'm going to work." She headed for the bathroom and slammed the door behind her.

"You're just going to walk out?" he shouted. "What about us? What about what happened here? You think you can forget what we shared?"

That was exactly what she hoped to do. Maggie tugged her jeans over her hips, forgetting about underwear. Then she pulled a sweater over her head and ran her fingers through her tangled hair. "And what happened here? This was just a...a fling. We got carried away. We satisfied our curiosity. That's all."

"No, there's more, Maggie. I felt it in the way you touched me, I saw it in your eyes. You can't deny it."

She swung the door open and stalked back into her bedroom. To her relief, he'd pulled on his own jeans, but they were unbuttoned at the waist, riding dangerously low on his hips.

"Once again, you're not giving me any credit," she said. "I knew perfectly well what I was doing when I crawled into bed with you. And I know what I'm doing now."

"You're running away," he said. "That's typical. You never want to stay around and take a chance. If it doesn't fit into one of your little plans, you turn and run."

"And what's going to happen if I stay?" she challenged.

"We won't find out unless you do," he replied.

"I know what will happen. Sooner or later, you'll start to think about work. You'll get restless and wonder what's going on in the world, what you're missing."

"That's not true. If you haven't noticed, I've had a hard time getting on that plane to Albania."

"But you will. It's like an addiction for you, Luke. At least I'm honest enough to see you for the person you are."

"I'm not the one who's leaving now."

"So what are you going to do? Are you going to quit your job and settle down? What then? Are you going to make an honest woman out of me?" Maggie knew her words were harsh, but she had to make him see the truth in his feelings. He could never give her what she really wanted. At least she was smart enough to admit it.

Luke didn't answer for a long time and she grew increasingly uncomfortable with the silence. With an impatient sigh, she crossed the room and grabbed her engagement ring from the bedside table and pushed it back on her finger.

"All right," he said. He slowly crossed the room and took her hand in his. "I'd hoped this would be more romantic, maybe with candlelight and champagne, but I'll give it my best shot." Luke dropped to one knee. "Maggie Kelley, marry me."

All the blood drained from Maggie's body, pooling in the vicinity of her ankles. Her heart refused to beat and she couldn't draw a decent breath. Her thoughts jumped back to Colin's proposal, so solemn and sensible. She'd said yes without a twinge of doubt, without a second thought.

But this proposal was different. First of all, it was completely unexpected. And second, it was based on passion and desire and need, not practical considerations. Every emotion that raged inside her told her to accept, but Maggie's common sense prevailed. Luke Fitzpatrick didn't want to marry her any more than she wanted to marry him! "Don't mock me," she said.

"I'm perfectly serious," he countered.

Maggie pulled her hand away and clutched her hands together, twisting Colin's ring around and around on her finger. This was not supposed to happen. Luke wasn't the kind of man to consider marriage. He didn't want a wife. Especially a wife who wanted a home and family—and a husband who showed up at the dinner table every night.

"Well?" he prompted. "I'm still waiting for an answer."

"That question doesn't deserve an answer," Maggie muttered. She reached over, grabbed his jacket from the chair and shoved it at him. Then she stepped around him and strode to the front door, grabbing her coat and van keys along the way.

He caught up to her and blocked her escape, but she brushed past him and walked out the front door, leaving him standing in the doorway, dressed in just his jeans. "Don't leave, Maggie. You can't just walk away."

"And you can't stop me." Without looking back, she hurried to her van and unlocked it with trembling fingers. Maggie heard a soft curse and then the sharp slam of her front door. She jumped slightly, the finality of the sound piercing her heart.

Drawing on her resolve, she said a silent prayer, hoping the van would start in the cold and she wouldn't be forced to go back inside. After a few tries, the engine rumbled to life and Maggie put it in gear.

It wasn't until she'd driven halfway to her shop that she realized what she'd done—and why she'd done it. She wasn't angry at Luke because of Colin's call. In truth, she wasn't angry at all. Luke had only done what he'd been doing since they'd met all those years ago, watching out for her. How could she fault him for something that came as naturally to him as breathing?

And his marriage proposal had been a feeble attempt to appease her anger. Maggie knew him too well. He'd never be happy unless he was out in the world, living on the edge, facing danger every day. All she could give him was an ordinary existence, something he'd rejected early in his life. She wasn't as exciting as rebel uprisings and government coups. She was just Maggie Kelley from Potter's Junction, Wisconsin. A woman who wanted things he could never give her.

Her fingers tightened on the steering wheel. Maybe it was good they'd made love. There would never be any doubts, any thoughts of what might have been. It *had* been—and it was wonderful. But now it was over. Someday, they could be friends again, but Maggie would need time to forget everything that had happened recently between them. Maybe it wouldn't take that long. After all, she'd forgotten Colin in just a few short days. But then, Maggie had never loved Colin Spencer.

And try as she might, she couldn't stop loving Luke Fitzpatrick.

THE FAMILIAR SCENT of roses drifted through the air as Maggie closed the door of the cooler. She pressed her palms against the glass and stared down at the tall buckets of cut flowers—daisies and lilies and clouds of baby's breath. She'd always loved fresh flowers, the feel of the petals against her skin, the smell of a summer garden on a cold winter's day, the beauty of a bud barely opened. But nothing could make her happy today, not even a vase full of cheery daffodils.

At the end of February, she'd have to close the door of her shop for the last time. Maggie knew she could find a job as a designer anywhere in town. Her work was well known and respected. But she wasn't sure she wanted to stay in Chicago, not after all that had happened here. And that little shop in Potter's Junction kept tugging at her thoughts.

Over coffee that morning, she'd called the real estate agent and inquired about the floral shop on Main Street. She was certain she could break the lease on her coach house and if she sold everything in the Clark Street shop, right down to the cash register, she'd have enough to pay her living expenses for a few months.

Maggie could start a whole new life, away from all the memories she'd accumulated in Chicago with both Colin and Luke. And she'd be at a safe distance, so she wouldn't be tempted to wait for Luke's call or search for his face on a crowded street. Maybe over time she could come to terms with what had happened with him. If friends could be lovers, then why couldn't lovers become friends again?

"Luke," Maggie murmured. Just the sound of his name on her lips brought back the memory of their night together in her bed. She had whispered his name over and over again as he'd made love to her, not quite believing they were really together. Even after she'd walked out on him, everything still seemed like a dream, as if it had all happened in some faraway fantasy world.

"Well, it's in the past," she said, pushing away from the cooler and grabbing the bucket of white roses from beside her feet. "He's probably on his way to Albania. And my plan for a new life starts right now."

But she knew she couldn't truly put the past behind her until she spoke with Colin. Maggie glanced down at her hand. She wasn't quite sure what to do with the ring. She had thought about mailing it back to Eunice, but it had been a gift from Colin. Perhaps he might want to try to return it to the jeweler, or give it to someone else. Or throw it in Lake Michigan. Etiquette claimed she could keep it, but Maggie didn't want to keep a ring for an engagement that had barely lasted a week.

She'd return the ring to Colin and, at the same time, put her problems with men in the past. It was a new millennium. Anything was possible. The celebrations had died down and the world had begun to realize nothing had really changed. Life went on, with all the same ups and downs and joys and heartaches. Resolutions had already been forgotten and all the predictions, dire as they had been, had been taken in stride and solved with time.

She'd even thought about contacting Isabelle—if she

was back in town—but didn't feel quite ready yet. If she understood what had happened with Isabelle and Colin, maybe in time she'd be able to forgive her friend's actions.

She set the bucket of roses on the work table, pulled one from the water and snipped half the stem off. Idly, she wrapped the remaining stem with floral tape, twirling the flower in her fingers. One by one, Maggie built a lush bouquet of perfect roses, completing a wedding order Kim had begun the day before.

Such an optimistic time, Maggie mused. She'd dreamed of her own wedding day, planned it all so carefully in her mind until every detail was perfect. She would have a bouquet just like this one, perfect roses clustered together so tightly the scent would drift up around her as she walked down the aisle.

Maggie sighed and slowly set the bouquet down. She'd hung on to the fantasy for so long it was hard to let it go. But she knew there would never be a husband or a family. She had never really wanted to marry Colin. And after Luke, no man could ever make her feel the passion she'd felt with him.

"I'm doomed," she muttered, dropping her head onto her hands. "Doomed to make wedding bouquets for everyone but myself."

The bell at the door jangled and Maggie stood up, wiping her damp hands on her apron. Business had been slow for a Saturday, with only three walk-ins and a handful of deliveries. Once the deliveryman picked up the wedding order, she'd be finished. As she stepped out of the back room, Maggie froze, her hands still clutched in her apron.

Luke stood at the counter, his gaze fixed on her, his expression indifferent. "I would have called first, but I didn't think you'd want to see me."

Her heart thudded in her chest, nearly drowning out his words. For a moment she couldn't speak. But then she drew enough breath to clear her throat. "No," she murmured. "I—I mean, I'm glad you stopped by." She glanced at the bags he carried. "So you're finally on your way to Albania? I thought you might have already left."

He took a step closer. "You're glad I stopped by?"

She nodded. "It—it gives me a chance to apologize. For what I said. I—I'm sorry, I didn't mean to get so upset. We've been friends for a long time. You didn't deserve that."

He sighed and smiled, then walked toward her. "Aw, Maggie, I'm sorry, too. I didn't mean to mess things up the way I did. I shouldn't have been so pushy." He drew her into his embrace and kissed her forehead.

Closing her eyes, Maggie leaned into the warmth of his body, the subtle strength and shelter of his arms. She had wondered if she could ever put things right with him, but she'd never thought it would be this easy—just a few words, a simple smile and all was forgiven.

"Then we're friends again?" Maggie murmured.

His hands stilled on her back and she heard a curse catch on his breath. Luke grasped her shoulders and gently pushed her back until he could gaze down into her eyes. "Friends?"

Maggie nodded.

His jaw went tight and he shook his head. "No, damn it. That's not good enough. I don't want to be your friend. I asked you to marry me and I was serious. I want you to be my wife."

"I can't be your wife."

Luke cursed out loud. "Why not? I've got everything

figured out. When I get back from Albania, I'll talk Tom Wilcox into assigning me stories here in the States. And if that doesn't work, the *Tribune* has been after me for years. I'd be putting in long hours, but I'd be home every night. I probably wouldn't get the recognition I get now, but I'd work my way up."

"Why would you want to quit?"

"For you. For us. Maggie, we can have a life together. I can make you happy."

She pulled out of his embrace. "But I can't make you happy. When we were kids, I used to listen to your dreams about traveling the world and reporting on important stories, stories that made a difference in people's lives."

"I can do that here," Luke insisted. "I love you, Maggie. I think I always have. And maybe, I always assumed you'd be there when I got around to settling down. But I almost lost you and I'm not willing to risk that again."

"But I can't marry you," Maggie murmured.

"Why not?"

"Because love just isn't enough," she said. "It won't be enough when you decide you gave up something you wanted because of me. We should both be able to have what we want without compromising."

"What the hell is wrong with compromise?"

"Nothing," Maggie said, "if you're doing it for the right reasons. But you want to marry me because you're afraid I'll marry someone else. And maybe I'd end up marrying you because I'd be afraid no one else will ever ask." She drew a long breath. "What if I promised I won't marry anyone else? That if you decide you still want to settle down in five or ten years, I'll still be here. Would you give up your job with the syndicate then?"

He paused long enough for Maggie to know his answer. She smiled and pressed her palm against his cheek. "Your dreams have been my dreams since we were kids, Luke. I know you better than anyone in the world and I know what you want from life. It doesn't include a wife and a family."

"Maybe you don't know me that well anymore, Maggie. Maybe you don't know me at all." He raked his fingers through his hair and ground his teeth. "But I know you. And I know why you're doing this. You're afraid."

"Of what?" Maggie asked.

"Of making all the same mistakes your mother did. But you don't have to be afraid, Maggie. You determine your own future. It's as simple as that."

She shook her head. "It's not that simple. I know what it's like to lose someone you love. I watched my mother go through it over and over again. And I'm not sure I could stand losing you. It would hurt too much."

"You're losing me now, Maggie."

"But we're still friends," she said.

"No, we're not. I can't be your friend. I won't be. I guess you could call this an ultimatum. It's all or nothing." He hefted his bags up onto his shoulder. "Take care, Maggie. And if you change your mind, give me a call. I'll be back in a few weeks."

With that, Luke turned and walked out of the shop. Maggie stood near the counter, her white-knuckled hand clutching the edge for support. She wanted to believe she'd done the right thing, letting Luke go. He couldn't really love her, could he?

This whole thing had started with her engagement to Colin. When Luke had realized he was going to lose her to another man, he'd reacted with some primitive male instinct. He only wanted her because someone else did. That's why he hadn't told her about Colin. He didn't want to lose.

And he hadn't lost this time, either. He'd go back to his life just as easily as he'd walked away. In a few weeks, he'd forget that he'd ever wanted her, that he'd gone so far as to propose marriage. Maybe, once or twice a year, he'd think back to the night they spent together in her bed. In the end, Maggie would slip back into that part of his life he took for granted.

No, only one person had lost in this whole mess and that was Maggie. She'd lost her best friend. She'd lost the only man she could ever love. And she'd lost any chance she had for a happy life.

All and all, she was glad she wasn't going to be alive when the next millennium rolled around.

MAGGIE TRIED not to think about Luke. For the rest of the morning, she threw herself into insignificant activity, cleaning the workroom from top to bottom, catching up on her filing and completing a precise inventory of the enclosure cards for floral arrangements.

Work would keep her mind off the events of the past week. The harder she worked, the easier it would be to put her feelings aside. Though she only had a couple of months left at the shop, she was determined to make a success of that time. She'd almost managed an entire five minutes without thoughts of Luke. Until Eunice Spencer's driver walked through the front door.

Maggie groaned, then buried her face in her hands. "Go away!" she called through her fingers.

The chauffeur approached, his footsteps crisp on the hardwood floor of the shop, his shoes polished to a high gleam. Maggie glanced up at the tall, distinguished man to find a small envelope held out in front of her nose. "What's this?" she asked.

Hamilton straightened, putting on an official air. "I've been asked to deliver this."

Maggie frowned. "What is it? Another bribe from Eunice." She snatched the envelope from him and rubbed it between her fingers. "If it's cash, it's not much. But then, maybe it's a check."

The only reaction from Hamilton was a subtle lift of the eyebrow. "The note isn't from Mrs. Spencer. It's from Mr. Spencer."

"Edward? Now she's got her husband running interference for their profligate son?"

"No, miss. The note is from Mr. Colin, the... profligate son."

Maggie's heart lurched and her hands froze. Colin was back! Already? She knew he'd come back sooner or later, but she hadn't prepared herself for the return of the runaway fiancé. At least he hadn't shown up in person. Leave it to Colin to know the polite method to worm his way back into her life.

Well, she wouldn't let him back in! As far as she was concerned, she and Colin had nothing to talk about. With a soft curse, she ripped the envelope open and scanned the note, scrawled in Colin's familiar hand. When she finished, Maggie sighed and shoved the note back at the driver.

"Your reply, miss?"

Maggie ground her teeth. "Here's my reply." She grabbed the engagement ring, yanked it off her finger and held it out to Hamilton. "Tell Colin Spencer I have nothing to say to him. I won't be meeting him at the Spencer Center. Tell him I wish him the best but I never want to see him or talk to him again and if he comes near me, I'll call the police. Got that?"

This time both eyebrows went up. "Miss, I think it would be best if you told him in person. I'd be happy to drive you over to the Spencer Center. The car is right outside."

"Just take the damn ring and tell him I won't meet him," Maggie said. She pushed the diamond into his hand then walked away. Halfway to the workroom, she turned around. "And another thing." She stalked back to the driver. "Tell him I hope he and Isabelle had a good time, but I never want to see *her* again either."

"Is that all, miss?" Hamilton asked.

Maggie crossed her arms over her chest and considered a few more choice comments she had for her former fiancé. "Yes. I mean, no! You can tell him one more thing while you're at it."

"And what would that be, miss?"

"You—you can tell him I'm in love with another man. With Luke Fitzpatrick. Tell him that!" If that didn't put an end to Colin's expectations, nothing would. Not that she really loved Luke. She'd already decided that wasn't possible. But Colin didn't know that.

"Is that all?" Hamilton asked.

Maggie nodded emphatically then watched as the chauffeur turned on his heel and headed toward the door. "Wait!" she called.

He slowly turned back to her. "Yes?"

"Take out the part about Isabelle. I don't want to bring her into this."

"As you wish, miss."

She crossed the store and held out her hand. "And give me the ring back. I'll mail it to Colin with a note. That would be the proper way to handle the matter, don't you think?" Maggie stared down at the ring and frowned. "No, that wouldn't be the way to do it. It might get lost in the mail. I should give it back to him in person."

"Perhaps that would be best."

"I'll do it now," Maggie said, gathering her resolve. "Let me get my coat and you can drive me. We'll put an end to this."

Hamilton waited patiently while she gathered her things, then he pulled open the front door and held it as she walked outside. She fumbled for her keys and locked the door, questioning her decision. Was she really ready to face Colin, to stand in front of the man who had turned her entire future upside down?

Hamilton pulled open the door of the limousine and helped her inside. When he took his place behind the wheel and pulled out into the traffic on Clark Street, Maggie sank back against the soft leather seats and closed her eyes.

"May I speak freely, Miss Kelley?"

Maggie glanced up at the driver and found him watching her in the rearview mirror. "You can say whatever you want," she warned. "But it's not going to change my mind."

"I've known Mr. Colin since he was a boy. His parents have always given him everything. They did their best to spoil him. But Mr. Colin wouldn't have any part of it. He has a good heart, miss. And I think you should give him another chance to prove that to you."

"I can't marry him," Maggie said, tipping her head back. "I'm in love with Luke."

"Then you should tell him that," the driver said.

Maggie frowned. "Tell him what?"

"That you're in love with...Luke."

Maggie's eyes went wide and she scrambled up to the forward seat. "Who said I was in love with Luke?"

The driver shrugged. "You did, miss. Just now. And earlier you mentioned it as well."

She couldn't have just said it! Not out loud and not

without a good reason. If she said it out loud, then she must have meant it, so surely it just popped out of her mouth without reservation. Oh, God, she did love Luke Fitzpatrick. Not in some wishy-washy, platonic, he's-like-a-brother kind of love. She loved Luke, so completely and irrevocably that it had become part of her subconscious thought. It was so deeply embedded in her heart and mind, nothing she did, no amount of time or distance, would change her feelings.

Maggie folded her arms over the back of the seat and groaned. "I've made such a mess of this. I didn't want to love him." She looked up at Hamilton. "You have to understand my past. My mother fell in love with anything in long pants."

"Love is a strange and powerful force, miss. We can't always choose who we love. Sometimes love just chooses us."

"That's what Luke said."

Suddenly, Maggie felt an overwhelming need to put an end to her engagement. Once she was free of her past, she could look to her future, a future she wanted to begin today! She glanced at her watch and wondered if Luke had left for Albania yet. She didn't want to wait three weeks for his return. The longer she had to think about it, the more her determination would be tested.

She loved Luke Fitzpatrick and she was willing to do anything to spend the rest of her life loving him. How could she have been so blind? He'd been the most important person in her life for years and years and yet she hadn't had the good sense to trust him. To trust his love.

Sure, he was stubborn and pushy and he sometimes treated her like a child. But her happiness had always been first and foremost in his mind—and his heart.

And she'd just thrown it aside, like a childhood toy she'd somehow outgrown.

"I have to make things right," Maggie murmured. "If it takes me forever, I have to make it right."

10

LUKE STOOD in front of his desk at the syndicate offices and tossed an empty box onto his chair. He grabbed the photo of himself and Maggie he kept next to his computer terminal and stared at it. It had been taken a few years ago at the State Street ice rink by a photographer who worked for the syndicate. Maggie looked so pretty with her hair tucked beneath a slouchy hat and her nose red from the cold. He held her around the waist, her head resting against his shoulder, her fingers splayed across the front of his Blackhawks sweater.

Luke smiled. The two of them looked as if they belonged together, as if they'd been a happy couple for years. He remembered the afternoon the picture was taken, how he'd slipped his arms around her without even noticing what it felt like to touch her, how she'd pressed up against him without causing any reaction in him at all.

Now, every time he thought about putting his hands on her body, drawing her closer, he'd get lost in a flood of memories both vivid and vague, painful and pleasurable. How long had he loved Maggie? His feelings were so strong now, he must have loved her for a long time without even realizing.

Luke had never thought a whole lot about love, but now he could think of nothing else. He'd spent the past couple of days trying to figure out why he suddenly knew, without a shadow of a doubt, that he and Maggie were destined to spend the rest of their lives together. Maybe there was something to this millennium stuff, a convergence of planets or some shift in the cosmos. Or perhaps, it all came down to the prospect of losing Maggie to a guy like Colin Spencer. Whatever it was, Luke wanted his life with Maggie to start now.

But no matter how much he wanted that to happen, Luke wasn't certain he could pull it off. How the hell had he managed to mess things up so badly? He knew her refusal to recognize their love had nothing to do with Colin—or with the phone call Luke had neglected to mention. No, Maggie's fears ran much deeper, to doubts she had buried inside, from her childhood. Her instinct to protect herself was strong and if she felt even the tiniest sense of betrayal at Luke's behavior, she'd use it as an excuse to run away.

That's why she'd so stubbornly refused to step beyond the bounds of friendship. If she didn't love him, she didn't have to worry about getting hurt. Hell, she'd agreed to marry Colin Spencer and she'd never loved him.

His mind replayed his own proposal and Luke muttered a soft oath. He should have waited until Maggie had come to realize the true depths of her feelings. But Luke was never one to beat around the bush, never one to avoid the hard questions.

Her refusal still stung, but he couldn't blame her for turning him down flat. What woman would have said yes to such an offhand demand for a lifetime commitment? He was supposed to pledge his eternal love, then present her with a diamond worth at least a year's salary. And if she still wasn't convinced, he was supposed to offer her the moon and the stars and a four-bedroom house in the suburbs.

Hell, life would have been so much simpler if Colin

hadn't run out on her! If their engagement had actually been announced. Luke knew it was only his frustration talking. He owed a big debt to Colin Spencer's cold feet. What if Luke had realized his feelings for Maggie *after* she'd married Spencer? What would he have done then?

"What the hell are you doing back here?"

Luke looked up from his desk in the center of the newsroom, squinting through bloodshot eyes. Tom Wilcox stood a few desks away, his arms crossed over his ample chest, a scowl on his face. His boss's booming voice hurt Luke's ears and didn't do much to soothe the headache that throbbed in his temples.

"You're supposed to be in Albania!"

"I got there, then I decided to come home. The weather just didn't suit me." Luke picked up a hastily scrawled letter of resignation and held it out to his boss. "Here," he said. "This will make it official."

Wilcox snatched the letter from Luke's fingers and gave it a cursory read. "What about Janaz?"

"I called Jack Fischer and had him meet me at the airport in Athens. I gave him all the background material and then sent a message to Janaz that Jack would be coming in to do the interview." Luke reached for another stack of books and placed them inside the box. "Fischer is good. He'll give you a solid story."

Tom sighed and rubbed his balding head. "Have you lost your mind?"

Luke shrugged. "I don't know. Maybe. I've been on a plane or in an airport for nearly thirty-six hours straight. Right now, I'm not thinking too clearly so I'd only be guessing at my mental state."

"Then I'm not going to accept your resignation."

"Oh, no. I was quite lucid when I wrote that. I'm

done with this job, Tom. I've gone as far as I want to and now it's time to stop."

"So who got you? UPI or AP? What did they offer you? More money? A better travel allowance?"

Luke shook his head. He didn't want to have to defend his decision, but he realized an old reporter like Tom Wilcox wasn't going to let him get away without a full disclosure of the facts. "The truth is, nobody got me. I've just grown tired of living out of a suitcase eleven months of the year. I'm renting an apartment I never sleep in, I know the guys at Customs and Immigration better than I know my neighbors, and I've had to order new pages for my passport three times in the past two years."

"Tell me what you want," Tom said. "Is it money? More vacation time? Easier assignments?"

"I want a life. A life you can't give me. I want a real house I can come home to every night. And a job that doesn't involve automatic weapons fire." He glanced down at Maggie's picture and studied it for a long moment. "And I want a wife who loves me. Hell, I even want children." Luke slid the top drawer of his desk open and picked through the contents, tossing an autographed baseball and a hockey puck into the box.

"I'll give you an editorial position here," Wilcox said. "No travel."

Luke chuckled. "Nah, I don't think so. I need a fresh start. A new challenge." He put the last of his personal belongings into the box and closed the flaps. "I left all my files on Carter's desk. Everything else is on the laptop. If you have any questions, you can reach me at home."

The phone on Luke's desk rang and he glanced down at it, then back up at Wilcox. "You want to answer it or should I?"

Grumbling, his boss picked it up and muttered a gruff hello. A few seconds later, he shoved the phone at Luke. "It's some guy named Spencer. Says it's urgent."

Luke stared at the phone, not sure he should take it. He'd been trying to put Colin Spencer out of his mind and he'd hoped, out of Maggie's life. But Spencer's return was inevitable. Why now? He and Maggie were at a turning point in their relationship. The last thing he needed was Spencer back in the mix.

Luke didn't bother with a cheerful greeting. "What do you want, Spencer?"

"I know you probably don't want to talk to me right now and I don't blame you. But I figured we have a few things left unresolved between us."

"I don't have anything to say to you. Not after what you did to Maggie."

"I know how much you care about her but—"

"You know? No, I don't think you do. I love her," Luke said. "Do you understand? I want to marry her and if you think I'm going to let you anywhere near her, you've got another guess—"

"Shut up, Fitzpatrick, and listen. I've already talked to Maggie and we've straightened everything out between us."

Spencer's words tore through Luke's heart like a sniper's bullet. "What are you saying? She'd never agree to marry you. I know her. She wouldn't do that."

"I'm saying if you really love Maggie as much as you say you do, you'd better get off your butt and do something about it. In the meantime, there are a few things you should know."

If he could have reached through the phone and grabbed Spencer by the neck, he would have. Right now, he felt like planting a fist squarely on the jerk's pretty nose. Who the hell did he think he was? "I'm listening."

"I don't know if Maggie mentioned this or not, but she gave up the lease on her Clark Street shop. She was planning to move the business into a retail space in the lobby of the Spencer Center."

"How cozy for you," Luke muttered. But as he listened to Colin explain Maggie's business woes, Luke began to realize his old friend was no longer the enemy. Whatever feelings Spencer had harbored for Maggie had mellowed into simple concern for her happiness—happiness he believed only Luke could provide.

"So, that's it," Colin finally said. "That's all I wanted to say. From now on, it's up to you."

Luke drew a deep breath, unable to believe Spencer had given up without a fight. "Thanks."

"You don't need to thank me. It was the least I could do. And maybe after things are all settled we could get together for dinner."

Luke heard a click on the other end of the line, then slowly dropped the phone into the cradle. He took a step back and rubbed his forehead, trying to decide what to do next.

"All right, Fitzpatrick, how about this? I promise to start assigning you stories closer to home. North and South America only."

"I'm not staying," Luke repeated distractedly.

"North America," Tom countered.

"I'm not staying." Luke tucked the box under his arm and held out his hand. "Thanks for everything, Tom. For all the opportunities and the encouragement. I'm going to miss this place."

"All right," Tom called as Luke strode toward the

door. "The continental U.S. I can guarantee you'll be home three nights a week. How about that?"

Luke waved over his shoulder and pushed through the glass door of the syndicate offices. To his surprise, he didn't feel a single twinge of regret as he rode the elevator to the street level. He'd spent his entire professional career working for Global Press Syndicate, starting out as a copy boy and working his way up to a spot as their top international reporter. He was giving up a job he'd dreamed about from the time he first decided to be a journalist.

It didn't matter. If everything turned out the way he wanted, Luke Fitzpatrick would have a whole lot more than a coveted byline and a tattered passport. He'd have a life with Maggie Kelley, an endless string of mornings waking up beside her and of nights making love with her. He'd be able to listen to her voice for hours, to hear all her thoughts on every subject under the sun.

But first he'd have to get Maggie to admit she loved him. He'd never been an expert on romance, but he knew convincing Maggie of something she didn't believe could prove nearly impossible. The woman had planned her life out every step of the way, from the time she was a little girl. And once she decided on a course of action, there wasn't much—short of a nuclear explosion or a runaway fiancé—anyone could do to change her mind.

There had to be a way to put himself into her plans, a way to make himself part of her future. He'd have to be careful. If she thought for an instant he was trying to run her life, she'd never admit her feelings for him. The choice would have to be hers and hers alone. She would have to realize what they had together was worth saving.

MAGGIE SEARCHED the ice rink for Luke, looking for his
familiar form, the old Blackhawks jersey he always
wore, the easy way he moved over the ice. She still
clutched the pink message slip in her hand. Kim had
given it to her as soon as she'd come into the shop that
morning. Maggie wasn't sure why Luke hadn't called
her at home or why he hadn't stopped by to see her.
But that really didn't matter now. He was back in Chicago, and she wouldn't have to wait long to tell him
how she felt.

When she couldn't find him on the ice, she scanned
the perimeter. She found him leaning on the railing on
the far side of the rink, his elbows braced, his gaze
fixed on her. She waved hesitantly, but he made no
move to join her. Instead, he just watched, his expression enigmatic. Drawing a deep breath, she started toward him, her mind whirling with everything she'd
left unsaid. Maggie wasn't certain how she'd begin,
only that she had to find a way to repair the damage
she'd done.

By the time she joined him at the railing, her heart
was pounding in her chest and her breath was coming
in quick gasps. The most she could manage was a
strangled hello. She swallowed hard and forced a
smile. "You're back early," she ventured. "How was
Albania?"

Luke still hadn't taken his eyes off her and she felt
uneasy beneath his unwavering stare. "I got there and
decided to come home."

"What about the assignment?" Maggie asked, grateful they could break the ice with talk of his work.

"I turned it over to someone else."

He seemed so cool and distant, not at all like himself.
"What did your boss say about that?"

"Doesn't matter," Luke replied. "I quit."

Maggie gasped, her breath leaving her lips and clouding in the frigid air. "You quit?"

He nodded. "Yeah. I figured it was time. I need to try something new. Get a fresh start. Take my life in a different direction."

Maggie braced her arms on the railing and stared out at the skaters. "I know how you feel. I—I've been thinking about making some changes, too."

"I know," he murmured.

"You do?"

"Colin called me yesterday. He said you two had talked. He also mentioned you're considering moving back to Potter's Junction to buy that floral shop on Main Street."

"It was just a thought," Maggie said. "I—I mean, I haven't made any definite plans."

"I think it's a great idea. Not that you should listen to my opinion. I know how you like to make your own decisions. But if you're looking for a change, Potter's Junction would definitely be it."

Maggie's heart twisted and she bit her bottom lip to still the emotion that trembled there. She wanted to look into his handsome face and recall every perfect feature. She wanted to touch him, to run her hands over his body until he whispered her name. Instead, she kept her eyes fixed on a spot in the distance, fighting to keep her feelings in check. "Then you think I should move."

"That's what I'm planning to do," he said. "It's time to get out of Chicago."

"Where are you going?" The words caught in her throat and her voice sounded unnaturally calm.

"I haven't decided. It all depends. I just figured I'd know when I got there."

A long silence grew between them. She'd never expected this. She'd come here believing with all her heart she could salvage the love they'd shared. But it was too late. She'd pushed Luke away once too often, and now he'd moved on. He was ready to start a new life, a life that didn't include her. "Then I guess this is the end," she murmured, stunned by the thought of losing him forever.

"Naw," he said, slipping his arm around her shoulders. "It's a new beginning. For both of us." He turned to face her, then grabbed her hands. "We'll always be friends, Maggie. That's what you want, isn't it?"

Her mind screamed an answer, silent but deafening. No! She didn't want to be friends! She wanted so much more. And how could he be so indifferent? How could he walk away after what they'd shared? He had told her he loved her. True love wouldn't just fade after a few days apart, would it?

She glanced down at her hands, her fingers linked together with his. Gently, she tugged them out of his grasp and turned her palm up. Slowly, she traced the little star at the base of her thumb. With a soft laugh, she held out her hand. "The mark of the millennium," she said, pointing to the little intersecting lines.

He took her hand again and brought it close, examining the spot. A shiver skittered down her spine at his touch. Maggie closed her eyes as he ran his fingertip along her thumb. She missed the way his skin felt against hers and they'd only been apart for such a short time. How would she be able to stand losing him for good?

"What does it mean?" Luke asked.

"That night, at the Millennium Eve Ball, a fortune-teller told me I'd marry the man I was with at midnight. He would be my destiny because I have this little mark. It didn't work out quite that way, did it?"

"How so?"

"Well, Colin ran off with Isabelle and—"

"You were with me," Luke finished.

"I was with—" The words died in Maggie's throat. She drew in a quick breath. "You." The word came out on a sigh and the realization hit her like a hard slap to the face. She'd been with *Luke* at midnight on the turn of the millennium. Could *he* be the man the fortune-teller had called her destiny? Had she completely missed the point? Maggie swallowed hard.

Suddenly, it all made sense. Everything that had happened since the hour of midnight on the millennium had been happening for a reason! Luke Fitzpatrick was her destiny—only she'd been too stupid to see it.

"It's just a few little wrinkles," he said, letting her hand drop. "You're the one who determines your future, Maggie. Not some fortune-teller. And I think you've made a good decision."

"What if I haven't?" Maggie asked.

He shrugged. "I suspect you'll know soon enough." Luke glanced at his watch. "I suppose I should go. I've got a lot of packing to do."

"No!" Maggie said. "Let's stay for a little while longer. I—I've got time."

Luke turned away from the railing and leaned back on it. He reached out for a box sitting on the end of a park bench and handed it to her. "Here," Luke said. "I was cleaning out one of my closets and I found this. Open it."

Maggie sat down on the bench and placed the box on her lap. "What is it?" She untied the tangled string holding the top. The tattered box looked vaguely familiar, but she hadn't a clue as to what was inside. Luke had never given her gifts, except for— A soft sigh slipped from her lips as she looked down at a well-worn pair of figure skates. "Where did you find these?"

"They were in a stack of stuff in the back of my bedroom closet. I'm not sure how they got there. I've helped you move so many times, I just figured I ended up with some of your things by mistake. I couldn't believe you hadn't thrown them out."

"They were a gift," Maggie murmured. "The first gift you gave me."

"The only gift," he said, shaking his head. "I haven't been a very good friend, have I?"

"I don't need gifts to prove we're friends," Maggie said. She ran her fingertips over the old leather. "I loved these skates. I wore them even after my feet got too big and the toes pinched. I didn't want to give them up. I used to believe there was magic in the blades, that they made me a better skater."

Luke picked up one of the skates from the box and carefully examined it, running his hands over the cracked leather and the nicked blades. They seemed so tiny in his hands and Maggie wondered when her feet had ever been that small, when her life had ever been so simple.

"Well, they're back where they belong. Maybe someday you can give them to your daughter. You can tell her all about your old friend, Luke."

Maggie felt the tears press at the corners of her eyes, then freeze in the cold air. When she imagined her children, she saw them with dark hair and blue eyes, just like Luke's. "I—I'll do that. And I'll pray she finds a friend as good and true as you were."

He drew a long breath, then smiled. "Are. I'll always be your friend, Maggie. No matter where you go, you know you can depend on me."

Maggie nodded. She didn't want him to leave but she couldn't ask him to stay. Maybe this was how it was supposed to be, the two of them going their separate ways in the new millennium. Maybe this unrelenting ache in her heart was her true destiny. She didn't want to believe it.

He bent closer and brushed a kiss on her forehead. "Take care," he said. "And when you get settled, drop me a line. The post office will forward my mail for a year."

With that, he stood up. Maggie's heart lurched. She wanted to scream and wail and beg him to stay. And though her heart was being torn in two, her mind still refused to give in to emotion. Luke was walking out of her life. For good. If he truly loved her, he would have done anything to be near her.

She turned away, unable to watch, unwilling to let her last memory of him be this terrible image. How could it have all gone so bad? She'd finally found a man she could love, a man who brought passion and desire into her life, as well as happiness and contentment. Surely this couldn't have all happened for nothing.

She pressed her hands into her lap and stifled a sob. "Maybe it is in your genes, Maggie Kelley," she murmured. "After all, you are your mother's daughter."

MAGGIE BRUSHED a damp strand of hair from her eyes and straightened, working at a kink in her back along the way. She'd been scrubbing the old tile floor of her new shop since early that morning and her hard work was beginning to pay off. The Northwoods Florist would be open for business in a week. She'd already placed her first order for fresh flowers with the wholesaler and two brides had stopped by to discuss wedding arrangements.

Once the shop was in order, she could start to work on arrangements for the windows and the interior displays. And she'd already contacted the local community college about teaching a night class in flower gardening. All in all, her plan was coming together quite nicely.

She'd left Chicago over a month ago, moving herself and what was left of her business to Potter's Junction. At first, she'd been certain it was the right move. She had vowed to work hard and forget Luke. They'd still stay in touch, but it was different now. Too much had passed between them, too many words they couldn't take back. They couldn't be the kind of friends they used to be. Becoming lovers had changed all that.

Though their lives had gone in different directions, Maggie knew he'd always occupy a place in her heart. Maybe he'd come and visit or they'd talk again on the phone. She didn't want to believe she'd never hear his voice again.

She glanced at her watch, then dropped the rag in the bucket and stripped off her rubber gloves. She'd decided to place an ad in the *Lake Country Register*, announcing the grand opening of her store. But the newspaper offices had been closed for the past few days. No one had bothered to return her phone calls, so she'd made a habit of stopping by on her way home for lunch.

Maggie grabbed her jacket from the counter and tugged it on, then retrieved the file folder that held her new logo and the ad she'd designed. It was critical that she got good publicity right at the start. She hoped Cal Winslow would agree to do a feature on her new business, so everyone in town might feel compelled to stop in.

The newspaper office was just a block away and she walked quickly through the frigid wind that buffeted her body. When she arrived at the door, she half expected it to be locked again. But when she turned the knob, the door opened and she stepped inside.

She walked up to the front counter and cleared her throat, but nobody appeared there to help her. A little bell sat near her right hand and she gave it a tap and then another. She was about to leave, when she heard a voice call from the back.

"I'll be right with you!"

Her heart stilled and her breath stopped. That voice! An unbidden flood of emotion washed over her. It sounded just like Luke. Maggie pinched her eyes shut and scolded herself silently. Every man seemed to sound like Luke lately. She heard him at the hardware store and in the post office. She even thought she'd seen him on the street the other day. Never mind all the times he'd appeared in her dreams.

"Can I help you?"

Maggie opened her eyes. But the man standing before her was just another dream. She blinked, then rubbed her eyes, but the vision of Luke refused to disappear. Only after she saw him smile was she willing to believe he was real.

"Did you just stop by to stare," he asked, "or was there something you needed?"

She tried to speak, but nothing came out. Finally, she was able to catch a decent breath, but all she could manage was his name. "Luke."

"Maggie."

"Luke?"

"Maggie?"

She wanted to reach out and touch him, to throw herself into his arms and rain kisses over his face, just to prove to herself he was real. But the sound of his voice, the beautiful blue of his eyes and the scent of his aftershave were proof enough. "Wha—what are you doing here? Have you come for a visit?"

Luke shook his head. "I bought the paper."

His words sounded so matter-of-fact, as if he'd just told her he'd had a cheeseburger for lunch. "You what?"

"I bought the *Lake Country Register*. Cal Winslow was looking to slow down a little. So I agreed to buy him out. He still works here. I'll need him if I'm going to publish three times a week and he's—"

"I don't understand," she interrupted. "Why would you come here? To Potter's Junction?"

"Opportunity," Luke said. "Yeah, that's it. There are a lot of opportunities up here. Now, what can I do to help you, Maggie? Are you interested in buying an ad? I heard your shop will be open next week. The *Lake Country Register* can put that news right in the laps of your customers. And for a very reasonable price, I might add."

Stunned, Maggie wasn't sure what to say. There were so many questions she had, so many hopes and so many anxieties. Had he followed her here? Was she the reason he'd returned to Potter's Junction? Was there a chance he still loved her?

"Maggie?"

"Oh, yes! The ad." She shoved the file folder across the counter and waited as he opened it, studying him covertly. He hadn't changed. If anything, he'd grown more handsome in the past month. Her hands clenched as she remembered the feel of his hair in her fingers, the taste of his mouth on her lips. She was tempted to lean over the counter and drag him into a mind-numbing kiss. If she kissed him, she was certain she'd understand his motives. Maggie reached out. But then he looked up and she drew back, losing her courage.

"This looks like five inches by two columns," he said. "Are you sure that size will be big enough?"

"I—I don't know," she said, her heart pounding in her chest. "How much will it cost?"

Luke grabbed a piece of paper from beneath the counter. "Hmm. An ad this size will run you about…seven hundred and ninety-five dollars. That's for one placement."

Maggie gasped. "What?"

A grin curled his lips and he shrugged. "But since you're an old friend, I guess I could give you a discount. How about seven hundred and fifty dollars?"

"For one ad? In the *Lake Country Register?* That's more than my monthly mortgage payment on the shop! I can't afford to advertise at those rates."

"Well, if you were my wife, I could probably cut you a better deal."

This time, her breath didn't leave her body. But her knees went weak and Maggie clutched the edge of the counter for support. Had she heard him right? Did he still want to marry her? She swallowed hard. "Your wife?"

"Yeah. If you were my wife, I could give you the ad for free."

"I—I don't understand."

"Aren't I making myself clear?" He slowly circled the end of the counter, then stood in front of her. "I came here and bought this place because of you. This is where you were and I didn't want to be anyplace else. Maggie, this is the perfect place to grow old together.

And a good place to raise a family." He took her hands in his. "Now, I know it might take a while to convince you, but if you're planning on a big advertising schedule, you might want to make a decision soon."

"A decision?"

"What's it going to be? Will you marry me, Maggie Kelley?"

Maggie couldn't speak, hope and joy welling up inside of her, blocking her throat. A tear slipped from the corner of her eye. He still loved her. Everything standing between them, tearing them apart, had crumbled in this single instant.

Luke wiped the tear away with his thumb. "Maggie, I never thought much about settling down and having a family. It just didn't fit in with the life-style. But when I thought about spending the rest of my life without you, I couldn't breathe. I think I've always loved you. I'm not sure when it happened. Maybe—"

"That day you picked me up off the sidewalk after that bully knocked me down," Maggie said. "That's the day I fell in love with you."

He smiled and drew her into his arms. "My life has been wrapped so tightly around yours for so long that I can't pull us apart anymore. I used to be able to, but I can't now. And I don't want to."

"I don't want that, either," Maggie murmured, her heart nearly bursting with joy.

Luke took her face in his hands. "I asked you to marry me, Maggie. And if it takes me the rest of my life, I'm going to convince you to say yes. I can't do that if I'm half a world away."

Emotion clogged her throat. "Yes," she said, the word coming out in a whisper.

"Yes?"

"The answer is yes," Maggie said.

His jaw dropped and he stared at her for a long moment. "Just like that? Yes?" Then a lazy smile curled his lips. "You're saying yes?"

Maggie giggled through her tears, wrapping her arms around his neck. "How many times do you need to hear it? Yes. Yes, yes, yes!" Her words echoed through the newspaper office. "Yes, Luke Fitzpatrick, I will marry you!"

Luke laughed as he pulled her into his arms. "God, Maggie. I love you so much!"

He twirled her around and around, then finally put her back on her feet. But Maggie couldn't feel the floor. She felt as if she were floating on a cloud, lost in a dream. When Luke finally stopped kissing her, she stared up into his eyes.

Something magical had happened that night when the new millennium began. A whole new life had opened up in front of her. She'd been so afraid to take the first step, to let herself love Luke. But now that she had, Maggie realized the prophecy had been right all along.

She'd stared into the eyes of destiny that moment at midnight. And destiny's eyes were a pale blue. And his hair was dark and thick. And his words had the power to touch her soul and capture her heart.

Luke Fitzpatrick was her destiny and together they'd make a wonderful life together in a brand-new millennium.

COMING NEXT MONTH

#761 A BABY FOR THE BOSS Jule McBride
Bachelors & Babies

Sexy, macho hostage negotiator Rafe Ransom was forced to
undergo sensitivity training by looking after the baby of his
assistant McKinley! Soon he found himself bonding with the
little boy—and figuring out how to bed the feisty and beautiful
mom. Then he learned McKinley had *ulterior* motives....

#762 ALWAYS A HERO Kate Hoffmann
Millennium Book II

Colin Spencer, heir to the Spencer fortune, never knew what hit
him. While en route to the party where he'd announce his
engagement, he found himself stuck on the elevator with sexy
Isabelle Channing and a bottle of bubbly. Next thing he knew, he
was a married man. Which wouldn't have been so bad, except
that he'd married the wrong woman. Or had he?

#763 BACHELOR BLUES Leanna Wilson

Wade Brooks wasn't looking for everlasting love—but he
definitely needed a little female companionship. He wanted
someone safe, someone *comfortable*, and Jessie Hart's dating
service seemed to be the answer. Only, the sizzling sexual
attraction between Wade and the sultry brunette was making
Wade decidedly *un*comfortable....

#764 ALL OF ME Patricia Ryan
Blaze

David Waite had been burned once too often by women who
pretended to care for him while profiting from his society
connections. His solution? "Arm candy"—a beautiful woman to
accompany him in public, no strings attached. Nora Armstrong
was perfect.... Maybe too perfect, because David found himself
wanting to change the rules....

CNM1299

EXTRA! EXTRA!

The book all your favorite authors are raving about is finally here!

The 1999 Harlequin and Silhouette coupon book.

Each page is alive with savings that can't be beat!

Getting this incredible coupon book is as easy as 1, 2, 3.

1. During the months of November and December 1999 buy any 2 Harlequin or Silhouette books.

2. Send us your name, address and 2 proofs of purchase (cash receipt) to the address below.

3. Harlequin will send you a coupon book worth $10.00 off future purchases of Harlequin or Silhouette books in 2000.

Send us 3 cash register receipts as proofs of purchase and we will send you 2 coupon books worth a total saving of $20.00 (limit of 2 coupon books per customer).

Saving money has never been this easy.

Please allow 4-6 weeks for delivery. Offer expires December 31, 1999.
